GOOD NIGHT, GRINGO...

As they entered the cooler darkness of the downstairs cantina, Gaston suggested, "Wait, let us enjoy a bracing drink before we march upstairs to meet our makers, non?"

Captain Gringo chuckled and said, "Good thinking. But where the hell *is* everyone? This place has to be open for business by now, right?"

A totally strange voice said, "Wrong," behind him, and before the sleepy Captain Gringo could come unstuck someone dropped at least a steam locomotive on him!

As he hit the hard tile floor with his knees, hard, he heard Gaston shouting something from far far away....

Novels by
RAMSAY THORNE

Published by
WARNER BOOKS

Renegade #33

COSTA RICAN CARNAGE
Ramsay Thorne

WARNER BOOKS

A Warner Communications Company

WARNER BOOKS EDITION

Copyright © 1985 by Lou Cameron
All rights reserved.

Cover art by Samson Pollen

Warner Books, Inc.
666 Fifth Avenue
New York, N.Y. 10103

 A Warner Communications Company

Printed in the United States of America

First Printing: December, 1985

10 9 8 7 6 5 4 3 2 1

After spending a night with Melina, Captain Gringo had to get up so he could get some sleep. As he eased his bare buttocks off the mattress, the treacherous bedsprings ratted on him. The voluptuous Melina rolled over and reached absently for him. Captain Gringo quickly gave her a hand to play with. So Melina moved it back in place aboard one of her heroic breasts with a contented sigh and proceeded to snore some more. Melina's snoring was on the heroic side as well. That was why it was impossible to get any sleep in the same room with her. When the tawny would-be blonde wasn't screwing like a mink, she was snoring like a buzz saw and, all in all, it had been a long night.

Captain Gringo waited until her snores settled into a steady crosscut before he gently removed his hand from her soft warm flesh, made it this time, and padded barefooted across the morning-cold tiles to the washstand in the corner. The water was cold too. Everything in the posada but Melina felt cold and clammy in the tropic dawn, even though the sunlight glancing through the window jalousies promised that the day to come would be a scorcher. Old tropic hands like the young American renegade knew better than to skip a morning whore bath, no matter how cool a dry season day might dawn, unless they just didn't care what the neighbors thought about their sex lives. The sleeping enchilada across the room smelled sort of yummy at the moment, but he had noticed when they'd met in the first cool shades of the previous evening that her perfume was getting a little gamy, and they'd done some sweating together indeed aboard those rumpled sheets, despite the trade winds wafting gently across their naked bodies as they got to know each other better.

He washed his privates and under his arms. Then he gave himself a quick once-over with the clammy washrag, dried himself as dry as one could get in the prevailing humidity of the Costa Rican lowlands, and slipped into his wilted linen duds, planter's hat and gun rig. He thought he'd better just hang on to his mosquito boots until he was out of earshot. He thought he'd made it. But as he opened the door out to the balcony, Melina stopped snoring and sighed. Captain Gringo sighed too. You couldn't trust some dames, even when they were snoring. Melina ran a groping hand over the dent he'd left in the pillow next to hers and pouted, "Ah, querido, where are you? I feel so passionate!"

He murmured, "Hold the thought. I'll be right back."

It didn't work. Melina opened one eye, saw him fully dressed in the doorway, and opened the other as well, to demand, "Where do you think you are going, you cruel thing? Is this how a gentleman treats a lady after using and abusing her? I knew you would desert me once you were weary of toying with my emotions!"

He smiled crookedly down at her and replied, "Go back to sleep. How can a guy desert a dame stretched out in his own bed? We're at my place, not yours, remember?"

"Si, I think so. I am somewhat confused as to just what happened after that last gin and tonic. I recall going to bed with you, you naughty thing, but . . . if you are not trying for to get rid of me, where are you going, ah, was it not Ricardo?"

"My friends call me Dick. I have a few morning errands to attend to. I'll be back in a while. If you're still here, we'll probably act naughty some more. So go back to sleep."

Melina sat up instead and insisted, "I feel naughty *now*. Can you not fuck me good morning at least before you have to rush off?"

Captain Gringo was tempted, even though she'd already wrung him out like a dish rag with her warm, pulsating flesh and then kept him awake the rest of the time with her awesome snoring. She wasn't snoring right now, and the tiger stripes of sunlight on her smooth brown flesh made her awesome curves look even more awesome. He knew by the part in her shoulder-length hair that she wasn't really a blonde. But her exact natural shade was up for grabs because of the way she shaved or plucked her pubic hair, and the results were very nice to grab indeed. But he didn't want to go through washing and getting dressed again so soon. So he blew her a kiss, stepped out on the second-story balcony, and took off before she could leap out of bed at him.

He and his sidekick, Gaston, had booked rooms next to one another at the posada in the native quarter of Limón. So, to clear the long balcony pronto, Captain Gringo ducked into his pal's digs, knowing that the dapper little Frenchman hadn't come home from the Paseo the night before. That is, he knew it until he burst in on Gaston and two girls he should have been ashamed of sleeping with. One was black and one was more or less white. Neither could have been over sixteen, and Gaston Verrier, late of the French Foreign Legion, was probably fibbing when he admitted to being sixty or so. As Captain Gringo froze, bemused, near the foot of the brass bedstead, Gaston opened one eye to remark, calmly, "Eh bien, you are just in time for breakfast, my insatiable child. One assumes you wore that poor blonde out by now?"

Captain Gringo chuckled and replied, "I'm not sure who wore whom out. I was hoping to kip out in here till you crawled home. I guess the three of you came in sort of quietly, eh?"

"Merde alors, we could have been blowing bugles and *you* would not have noticed, Dick. What was that blonde screaming about, around three A.M.?"

"What do dames getting laid at three A.M. usually scream about? I'm too tired to gossip about the unfair sex, Gaston. I have to find a place to catch forty winks."

The black girl resting her head on Gaston's shoulder opened her eyes, fixed him with a bleary smile, and murmured, "Oh, nice! Are we going to have a party?"

Gaston agreed that that sounded like a grand idea. Captain Gringo crossed the room and yanked open the hall door before anyone could yank him into yet another rumpled bed. As he did so he spied an envelope on the doorsill, and all bets were off. He bent to pick it up, muttering, "How the hell could *we* be getting mail, Gaston? I thought you told me that this posada was safe."

Gaston snorted and said, "Merde alors, of course it is safe. If it was not safe, nobody would be shoving messages under our doors. We are not currently wanted here in Costa Rica. Even if we were, I can't see la policia communicating with us in such a civilized manner, hein?"

Captain Gringo nodded thoughtfully and turned the officious sealed envelope over to read his own name rather than Gaston's on the address side. When he commented on this, Gaston said, "Eh bien, whoever put it there mixed up our room numbers. Would you either come in or go out, Dick? I am a man of the world, as you know, but I do not wish to be seen from the hall in this delicate position."

Captain Gringo glanced his way, saw what he meant, and stepped out in the hall to shut the door as the now wide-awake young Negress went down on the gray, but surprisingly virile, old man.

Captain Gringo went down the stairs, saw that the cantina on the ground floor wasn't serving drinks yet, and sat at a corner table near an open window to open the envelope.

The message was officious too. It told him there was a package waiting for him at the general post office across town. They had his name right. It still didn't make much sense. The former First Lieutenant Richard Walker of the U.S. 10th Cavalry wasn't used to getting packages or even mail since he'd fled the States one jump ahead of an Army hangman's noose. It had to be a mistake, or perhaps a bomb. A lot of people were after him these days. He hoped his friends and relations back home in Connecticut thought he was dead. He'd been reported dead a lot in his more recent career as a soldier of fortune, and in any case, few people back home should connect the notorious Captain Gringo with that nice boy next door who'd gone off to fight Apache and never returned.

He stuffed the notice in his pocket and lit a Havana Claro

as he pondered his next move. He was still bone-tired but now wide-awake, and he knew he'd never be able to fall asleep until he solved the mystery. So he cursed, got up, and went out to trudge his weary way to the fucking post office.

It didn't take long. The little seaport of Limón wasn't all that big, no matter where you might find yourself in it. His stomach was starting to growl, but he found the post office open and decided to examine the mysterious delivery while he ate breakfast.

There were no other customers inside. The clerk on duty glanced at his notice, shrugged, and rummaged through a pile of packages to dig out the one addressed to him. It was wrapped in bright red paper. Captain Gringo noticed others in the pile as dramatic. Latins painted stucco walls all kinds of bright colors too.

He had to sign for it. That gave him pause, since he hadn't signed his right name for some time indeed. But on reflection, Old Gaston was right about their not being wanted in Costa Rica, and a police trap this involved made no sense in any case. The package was addressed to the posada he'd been staying at since returning to Limón, and he'd only been required to pick it up here in order to sign for its insured contents. Anyone who already knew where to find him would have no reason to lure him into a trap in the center of town. He and Gaston had chosen their more secluded current address because it was in a neighborhood where occasional gunshots didn't attract too much attention.

He signed, picked up the limp, bulky package, and carried it out and across the plaza to a sidewalk cantina serving food as well as drink. The waitress said he could have tortillas and beans with his cerveza or beans and tortillas with his cerveza. Just to be different, he ordered tortillas and beans and began to open the red package on the table as she went to fetch his order.

He wouldn't have opened it had not he been able to feel that whatever it was it was too soft and squishy to be a bomb. Before he could find out what it was, someone shoved something cold and hard against the nape of his neck and said, politely, "You will rise most slowly and come with us, Captain Gringo, unless you wish for to die here and now."

The tall American politely kept his hands on the tin table as he asked, conversationally, "Does that mean I get to die someplace not so public, or are you just taking your job seriously, amigo?"

A second voice replied, in a harsher tone, "We are not to be referred to either as motherfuckers or your *friend,* yanqui! Whether you die here or not is up to you. Whether you die after our patron has a word with you shall be up to *him!*"

"I guess we'd better go see your patron, then. Do I carry this package to him or would you rather do it yourselves, muchachos?"

"Leave it on the table. Get up and turn around most slowly, and do not make any more amusing remarks about us. We are serious men."

As he rose and turned he saw that they sure seemed to be. Both were well dressed albeit clad in the riding outfits of upland rancheros. The one holding the big Patterson Colt conversion on him reached inside Captain Gringo's jacket to relieve him of his own .38 double-action. Then he lowered his own weapon politely and said, "Bueno. You will come with us in a reasonable manner or, if you so choose, die anywhere between here and where we are all now going in a civilized way, attracting as little attention as possible."

Captain Gringo said, "Lead on, Macduff." So the other one picked up the package as the waitress came out to ask, "Do you not wish this breakfast and beer, señor?"

The one holding the package put some silver on the table as he explained politely that el señor had another morning appointment but, of course, intended to pay for his order. From the way she answered, Captain Gringo knew she'd been left a decent tip. Apparently the guy was only mad at *him.*

They frog marched Captain Gringo into an alley leading away from the plaza and then marched him through some others until at last they came to an oaken gate leading into a pepper-tree-screened pateo. Just inside, they met a severe old man with hair and beard to match his freshly pressed suit, and he seemed mad at him too. He slapped Captain Gringo across the face, with a riding quirt of course, to show that he was a true aristocrat, then told his boys to keep an eye on the dog as he took the package to a pateo table, sat down, and finished opening it.

He seemed surprised, too, when the contents proved to be several copies of last week's Prenza de Limón. He shoved the newsprint aside to light his own cigar thoughtfully. Then he looked up at the American and said, "I know they say you have a droll Yanqui sense of humor, Captain Gringo. But I do not find this joke at all amusing."

Captain Gringo said, "Neither do I. Suppose you let me in on it."

"Do you deny that this package was addressed to you or that my men just saw you coming out of the post office with it?"

"Not if your men saw me. I was wondering why it was wrapped in paper so easy to spot at a distance. Do you know who might have sent it to me, señor?"

The old man looked disgusted and said, "You know who I am. You know I sent the ransom you demanded as well, you loathsome kidnapper! I warn you, your death will be most unpleasant if you have harmed one hair on the head of my grandchild. And if she tells me you have trifled with her honor . . . well, I am still working on that. Nothing I have thought of so far could possibly be punishment enough."

Captain Gringo muttered, "Oh, boy!" then said, "You guys have the wrong guy if we're talking about a kidnapping. I'm a soldier of fortune, not a crook. What in hell gave you the idea I was in that other disgusting business?"

The old man glanced coldly down at the crumpled red paper and newsprint. Captain Gringo said, "Oh, right, you sent that fake bale of dinero to buy back some kid you're missing, and when I picked it up just now, you added two and two to get three. I don't even know who you are. So how the hell could I have kidnapped anyone from you?"

"It is no use for to lie, Captain Gringo. Nobody but us and, of course, the criminal holding my grandchild had any way of knowing I was to send that package to be picked up at the post office, and, by the way, I obeyed instructions and filled the package with real money, not old newspapers. So now we have something *else* to talk about, no?"

Captain Gringo shook his head and said, "No. You can see I never picked up the money you sent. Even *I* can see how someone just suckered us both. So why don't we cut the bullshit and go after the real son of a bitch before it's too late!"

Nobody else seemed awake yet. So he snorted in disgust and went on to explain, "You were told to wrap the ransom in red paper and send it to me care of the local post office. Meanwhile the sneaky bastards had already sent one, same red paper, same address, to you-know-who. They knew I'd show up first, claim the fake, and assumed all too correctly that we'd be having this dumb conversation while someone picked up the ransom money in a *later delivery*! Jesus H. Christ, don't you people down here have any con men? That's one of the oldest tricks of the trade!"

The old hidalgo studied the ash of his cigar as one of his gun slicks snarled, "How do we know you are not making up this fairy tale for to save your lying Yanqui head, eh?"

Captain Gringo said, "You won't, if you don't get someone to cover that post office some more, poco tiempo! Assuming the real ransom was mailed last night, in this neighborhood, it should have been picked up by now. The reason it wasn't there to meet me so early was that last night's pickups are getting sorted just about now. The decoy had to have been sorted *yesterday,* before you chumps mailed *anything,* see?"

The old man did. He snapped, "Hernando, get some of the others and cover the post office, *now*! Jose will stay here with me and our, ah, guest until you report back."

"What if the Yanqui is lying, Don Alberto?"

"I'll think of something. I told you to move. For why are you still *standing* there, Hernando?"

"I am not sure of my *patron*'s instructions."

"Jesus, Maria y José! You need instructions? Ask the clerk if another Ricardo Walker has picked up another package of any kind. If not, wait and follow the same game plan, you idiot! If we are indeed speaking of two packages, this young man may yet live. If we are not, we shall question him more harshly until he sees fit for to answer questions intelligently! Now go. Curse your mother's milk!"

Hernando went. Don Alberto grudgingly told Captain Gringo he could sit down now. The only place to sit was on the edge of a pateo fountain. But it beat standing. José still remained on his feet, the big Colt pointed at Captain Gringo as if he might be about to steal the goldfish.

A million years went by. A chica came out with refreshments for the old man. He didn't offer any to his prisoner or the man guarding him. But in slow grudging sentences Captain Gringo got a little more out of him.

The kidnap victim was his twenty-four-year-old granddaughter, the widow Lopez, who naturally was still under the protection of her clan, the high-country Montalbans of some cattle-raising fame. The name was familiar to Captain Gringo. He asked if he was correct in assuming that the stern family patriarch was a Spanish Basque. The old man looked at him as if he were stupid. So he said, "Right, I knew it was a Basque name. Some of my best friends are Basques. I don't like guys who break their word, either."

Grudgingly Don Alberto muttered, "We Basques know how to deal with dishonest people. Kidnappers are not even people to us. Such animals are to be put out of their misery, like the mad dogs they are. Do not try to flatter me, muchacho. If you have been telling me the truth, you have nothing to fear. If you have been lying . . . I am still working on it."

"Do you mind telling me just when, where, and how your grandchild was abducted, Don Alberto?"

"I do. If you had nothing to do with it, the matter does not concern you. If you did, you know, and I do not wish to be taunted about our family honor in even a veiled manner."

"Hey, what taunts? I'm as pissed as you are that someone suckered us into this dumb mess, Don Alberto! I'd like to help get the girl back if you'll let me!"

The old man looked away and murmured, "Nobody could be as pissed, as you put it, as myself. I have already given you the word of a Basque that you will live if it turns out you have, as you say, been sucked on. Beyond that, don't seek to gain my admiration. I know all too well about the notorious Captain Gringo. I know you are my guest at the moment. But beyond that, I do not associate with such people."

Captain Gringo chuckled and asked if it was all right to reach in his jacket for his own smoke. Don Alberto shook his head and told the guard to give him a cigar. That might have worked out better had José handed him one of the old hidalgo's perfectos. But the bastard reached in his own jacket for a cheaper brand. It could have been worse. At least José was polite enough to light it for him.

Captain Gringo didn't ask Don Alberto what he might have heard about him and Gaston. He knew. Some of the little people in Central America might approve of soldiers of fortune, but they tended to make the ruling class nervous as hell, with good reason. Costa Rica was run more fairly than most banana republics, but even here a little land reform couldn't really hurt. Unless you were one of the land hogs.

Another million years went by. It was getting hot now, even under the pepper tree's fluttering jade-green canopy. Captain Gringo got up to stretch. José followed his every movement with the muzzle of his revolver. So naturally José was at a tactical disadvantage when Gaston suddenly popped out of the wall shrubbery to shove his own gun muzzle into the small of José's back as he announced boyishly, "Eh bien, I've been looking all over town for you, Dick."

Captain Gringo disarmed José in one catlike move before

he answered. Then, as he helped himself to his own gun as well, he asked Gaston, "What kept you?"

The old man started to rise. Gaston told him, "Don't!" before he told Captain Gringo, "I had a little trouble finding this place, even with the return address to go by."

Then he reached inside his own jacket to produce a bright red package, adding, "There must be over ten thousand U.S. dollars in this package addressed to you, Dick. You never told me you had a très riche uncle."

Captain Gringo laughed and pointed at Don Alberto to say, "That's him. Give the man his money, Gaston. We're dealing with some kind of old switcheroo. Some dame's been kidnapped and . . . how the hell did *you* wind up with it, Gaston?"

Don Alberto snapped, "That was *my* first question, if you don't mind! How did this fellow ruffian of yours sneak that package from the post office without my men spotting him?"

Gaston shrugged, handed the even older man the red package, and asked, "Oh, were those unfortunate youths working for you? I assumed they were simply thieves when they attempted to take it from me, so . . ."

"Jesus, Gaston!" Captain Gringo sighed. But the deadly little Frenchman said soothingly, "Do not be alarmed. I did not have to kill any of them when they were kind enough to follow me into an alley of my own choosing. You say they were in the employ of this rather surly-looking gentleman? How curious that none of them could fight for merde. I left the four of them to sleep the effects of my feet off and hurried here to see where my long-lost child might be. As to why I picked it up at the post office, the answer is simple. I knew you had gone there to pick something up. When you failed to return, I was faced with the choice of servicing three raving sex maniacs or going out to find you. At the post office the clerk said you had in fact picked one package up but that now there was another for you in the mail just delivered. After some discussion and the exchange of a modest bribe, he graciously allowed me to sign for it. So the rest you know, hein?"

By this time old Don Alberto had the second package open and was counting his money with a glazed expression. As he was digesting that, the gate burst open, and four battered and no longer armed thugs came in all excited, then froze as they saw two gun muzzles covering them.

Don Alberto sighed wearily up at them and said, "I know. You were about to tell me that at least a hundred cutthroats jumped you and that you did not recover my money after all. May Hernando wash that ugly cut on his face in the fountain, Captain Gringo?"

The tall American nodded and politely lowered his gun to his side as he asked, "Is it over, Don Alberto?" You have your money back. So you have to be able to see that *we* weren't after it, at least."

"What about the real criminal who meant to pick up the second package in your name?"

"You'll play hell spotting him now. If it's not there to claim, he won't be coming out of the post office with it."

"But they say they mean to kill my grandchild unless they receive this very ransom, damn it!"

"What can I tell you? *You* didn't fuck it up. *They* did by trying to be too cute. They'll probably contact you again. I doubt that they'll suggest the same means of delivery next time. You said you wanted to handle it your own way. So good hunting. Let's go, Gaston."

The old hidalgo bleated like a sheep and said, "Wait! I am beginning to see that I may have misjudged you, young man!"

"You mean, you've noticed that the two of us are smarter and tougher than anyone you have working for you, don't you?"

"That too. How much would I have to pay you for to help me recover my poor little Teresa alive, señors?"

Before Gaston could get greedy, Captain Gringo said, "A handshake and such expense money as we might need to do it right."

Gaston wailed, "Dick, the man just mentioned *money*!"

But Captain Gringo shook his head and said, "Some cocksucker just tried to get me killed and, worse yet, ruin my reputation. You don't have to help if you don't want to, Gaston. It's not your beef. But if sure is *mine*. So I'm with these guys."

Gaston sighed, took out a clean pocket kerchief, and handed it to the cowboy bleeding on the goldfish as he said, "Eh bien, finding one no-doubt innocent maiden can't be as much work as trying to satisfy what's waiting to abuse me back at the posada. I'd better come along to keep you out of trouble, my impetuous youth."

Captain Gringo looked to see how Don Alberto was taking all this. The old man had risen soberly to hold out his hand. As Captain Gringo took it he said softly, "I see I *did* misjudge you, Captain Gringo. Tell me and my followers what must be done, and you have the word of a Basque that it shall be done, to the letter and to the death!"

The best-laid plans of mice and men gang aft aglae. Captain Gringo's first mistake was to say he was as hungry as a bitch wolf when their now much friendlier host suggested that they all go inside and have some breakfast while they discussed strategy. All Iberians tended to overdo feeding a guest, when they could afford it, and Basques seemed to think that they had a contest to win against mere Castilians. So Captain Gringo wound up talking with his mouth full most of the time, and toward the end, his tired brain was feeling bloated as well. Slabs of beef smothered in eggs and beans was not exactly what the doctor ordered to wake someone up who hadn't had any sleep the night before.

Captain Gringo said that he and Gaston should go back to the posada, get rid of the girls, and catch a few winks before they checked out. It hardly seemed likely that the kidnappers would try for another contact before they'd had time to figure out their own next moves. Don Alberto begged them not to leave, pointing out that he had oodles of guest rooms in his town house and demanding to know what he should do if the kidnappers contacted him before his newfound friends returned.

Captain Gringo belched and said, "If you hear from them this side of La Siesta, you'll know where to find us. I don't think they will. They couldn't know this soon that Gaston here fucked up the ransom delivery. When their man tried, or tries, at the post office, they're sure to wonder if the pretty red package may come in later in the day, after La Siesta. By then I may be making more sense, and we can see if any new instructions suggest a way to nail at least one of the bastards."

"Wait, the *first* ransom note warned me that any attempt on my part to rescue my grandchild would result in her most horrible death!"

"Sure it did. What would *you* tell a guy if you were holding his granddaughter for ransom? But saying and doing aren't always the same. If we have our own prisoner to act horrible with, they may have to revise their plans in a hurry. Whether we can force the info out of a gang member or not, the gang has to assume we might. So they'll have only two choices. They can swap their prisoner for ours, or they can kill her before they scatter. Either way they'll want to scatter, poco tiempo. You're a big man in this country. So they'll know that once the egg hits the fan, they'd better get *out* of it, right?"

The old man blanched and asked, "Are you suggesting that they might kill my poor little Teresa, Captain Gringo?"

"Hell, no, it was *their* idea in that first ransom demand, remember? Kidnappers come in two varieties. Ones who let their victims go unharmed and ones who don't. If we're dealing with old pros, they'll let your granddaughter live, not because they're nice guys but because it's smart. Costa Rica doesn't hang you for kidnapping. It does for murder, and if we have one of them, they can't be certain that they won't be caught in the end."

"Tell me about the other kind."

Captain Gringo had been afraid he was going to ask a question like that. He didn't know how to put it gently. So he shrugged and said, "If we're dealing with killers, we're dealing with killers. A killer doesn't need much excuse to kill. So, if they're planning on killing the girl, it hardly matters whether they get the ransom or not. Frankly, they may have already killed her. Some bastards would rather not be saddled with a possible screamer when they don't mean to leave a witness against them alive. But at least we can hope to bring them to justice if we can only capture one of them alive."

Don Alberto missed that last part. He'd leapt up to lean against the stucco wall and puke his breakfast all over it.

Captain Gringo got to his feet, walked over to him, and put a gentle hand on the old man's quivering shoulder. He said, "I'm sorry. That's the way life is. We'll be back around one. I know the siesta will have started by then. That's the point. If anyone's watching, they'll see Gaston and me return to our posada, and let's hope they'll assume we sorted our misunderstanding out and that's it. It's a bitch to watch or tail people during the siesta, when the streets are well lit and deserted. So we'll sneak back then, and we shall see what we shall see."

He nodded to Gaston, and the two soldiers of fortune left by the back exit. It wasn't anywhere near siesta time yet, but the alleyways they followed back to the posada seemed deserted and the sun so bright, they were starting to sweat by the time they got there.

As they entered the cooler darkness of the downstairs cantina, Gaston suggested, "Wait, let us enjoy a bracing drink before we march upstairs to meet our makers, non?"

Captain Gringo chuckled and said, "Good thinking. But where the hell *is* everyone? This place has to be open for business by now, right?"

A totally strange voice said, "Wrong." Behind him, and before the sleepy Captain Gringo could come unstuck, someone dropped at least a steam locomotive on him!

As he hit the tile floor with his knees, hard, he heard Gaston shouting something from far, far away. Then, as he tried to remember where the hell he kept his damned .38, that steam locomotive ran over him again and, what the fuck, he'd been planning on catching forty winks in any case, right?

When Captain Gringo woke up again, after some dreams that had been real pissers, he had no idea how long he'd been out, but he knew he hadn't had a good night's rest. For one thing it was broad-ass daylight, as far as he could judge from this position, and his head was hurting like hell. He shook his head, anyway, to clear it and finally figured out that he was belly-down across a pack mule with his wrists and ankles tied together by a horsehair riata running under the beast's belly. His own belly had to be draped over a hardwood pack saddle. No mule had two hard spines to dig into one's guts like that. He couldn't look up. But from the dappled sunlight on the red clay trail his face was dangling over, he could tell that they were out in the lowland jungle. Just *where,* of course, was up for grabs. There was jungle in every direction from the swampy coastline. If they'd still been at all near Limón, they'd still be in the more cultivated green belt around the seaport. He couldn't be sure, but they seemed to be going up a gentle grade. That figured. Who but an idiot would make camp on low ground in gator country?

By twisting his head slightly he could make out the rope-soled sandals of the bozo leading his mule. The toes were aimed away from him, of course. So that looked good. But when he twisted his head the other way, toes were pointing toward him in the company of a lowered shotgun muzzle. Ten gauge. Captain Gringo didn't know whether to feel flattered by all this attention or puke. From the taste in his mouth, he'd already puked a while back. So there was nothing to do right now but play possum until things got better.

Things got duller and more uncomfortable before they got better. He heard a distant voice cussing monotonously in French, Spanish, Arabic, and a couple of other languages. But when Gaston called out to him, he didn't answer. If Gaston was in shape to do anything about this ridiculous situation, he'd do it. Meanwhile, why tell their guards that both of them were now bright-eyed and bushy-tailed?

A few miles and a million years later, Captain Gringo heard a guitar strumming a sad gitaño tune in the distance. Naturally this seemed to cheer the damned mule up. So Captain Gringo got to ride into camp at a merry trot as he discovered how difficult it was for even an old cavalryman to post in the saddle on his gut.

He didn't get to see much of his new surroundings until they unlashed him from the mule, dumped him on his head, and kicked him when he tried to sit up. Then some jovial bully told the others to stop kicking him and haul him to his feet. So they did. He found himself staring into the face of what would have surely been a grinning Apache if they weren't all so far south. The Indian wore rings in his ears as well as ammo belts across his bare brown chest and a straw sombrero big enough for the average-sized Apache family to live in. He said, "So this is the most famous Captain Gringo, eh? Funny, I do not see the horns and tail I was led to expect. How come I see no horns and tail, Yanqui? You do not look so tough to me."

Captain Gringo shrugged as best as he could with his hands tied and said, "Nobody's tough when you have the drop on him. That's why I never talk tough to a man who can't fight back."

The Indian backhanded him across the face. He hadn't struck Captain Gringo as a good sport, even before he belted him. The bully growled, "Put him and the other big mouth with the puta for now. Make sure they are well tied and do not kill them before El Jefe returns for to have a last word with them.''

The guards grabbed Captain Gringo, spun him around, and frog-marched him toward a hut so recently built, its palm thatch was still green. Captain Gringo tried to size up the layout of the camp along the way. He wasn't able to see much that looked encouraging. He and Gaston met in the doorway. The Frenchman's mouth was bleeding, and one eye was swollen almost shut. Captain Gringo said, "After you, Gaston," but their handlers tossed them both inside on their faces, together. Fortunately Gaston wound up on top. As he rolled off, cursing, they both heard a woman sobbing somewhere in the gloom of the windowless hut. Gaston said, "Eh bien, ma petite. Let us begin by getting these très fatigué ropes off my poor old wrists.''

The girl stopped crying long enough to reply, "I can't. I'm tied to this old post." Then she started crying some more.

Captain Gringo told them both to shut up as he managed to sit up. He saw that the floor was red dirt, what else, and that the three of them seemed to be alone for the moment. But even thicker walls could have ears. So before Gaston could fuck up, he said, in English. "Eeway ontday owknay isthay ameday!" Then he asked her, in Spanish, who the hell she might be.

She sobbed, "I am Teresa Lopez. These terrible banditos kidnapped me, and they say if my family does not pay, they mean for to send me back to my grandfather one finger at a time!''

"Ouch. That could smart. How are your fingers and, ah, other parts so far?''

"If you are speaking of my honor, you do not know my people well. My maiden name is Montalban, and Basque women do not allow themselves to *live*, once they have been dishonored!''

"Yeah, well, don't commit suicide until they untie you at least. I'm Dick Walker, and this is Gaston Verrier. We don't have a grandfather between us. So do you have any idea why they might have wanted to kidnap *us*?''

He could see her better now, as his eyes adjusted to the dim light. Sure enough, she was seated upright against a post with her hands behind her. Her knees were exposed as well as dirty. Her once expensive dress of natural silk was dirty as well, and he was no doubt looking at more of her chest than she was used to showing in public. One shoulder strap was broken, and the only thing that kept that side of her bodice from falling all the way off her left breast was that said breast was big and firm enough to hold the top hem just above her nipple. The view from there up wasn't bad, either. Teresa Lopez was a little older than he'd expected from the way her grandfather had carried on about her. But she was still on the nice side of thirty, and he admired the way her long black hair framed her heart-shaped face. Her black brows were heavy above her nicely set sloe eyes. She looked too intelligent to be carrying on that way. So he told her, ''Simmer down and let's not waste our strength weeping and wailing. If they were going to kill us just for the hell of it, we wouldn't be having this conversation. How long have you been here?''

''Since the night before last. One moment I was sleeping in my own bed, alone, of course, and the next thing I knew, I was here. I think the chocolate I drank just before retiring may have been drugged. You know how treacherous servants can be.''

''I haven't ever had as many servants as you, I imagine. But I get the picture. Who's this grandfather of yours who you keep mentioning, señorita?''

''It is señora, por favor. I told you I was a married woman. That is, I used to be. Alas, the brutes took advantage of a poor helpless widow. My grandfather is Don Alberto Montalban, a most important ranchero near the capital with banana interests here in the low country as well. I am sure he will be willing to pay the ransom they demand. I know he has the money. Some of it is mine. When my husband died in a fall from his horse, the courts appointed my grandfather my custodian, of course."

Captain Gringo shrugged and answered, "Don't look at *me* like that. I never wrote the laws down here. Where I come from, dames are allowed to manage their own property. Last I heard, some of them were even demanding the vote."

Gaston said, "Eh bien, let us not waste time on Latin laws. I could not help noticing, señora, that your très attractive eyes seemed uncertain when you mentioned this distressing ransom business. Do you have reason to doubt that your family wants you back enough to pay for the privilege?"

Teresa looked away and replied, "I thought so, at first. I thought my grandfather loved me. But it has been so long now, and I've had so much time to think. I can't help wondering what would happen to my husband's estate if . . . We had no children, alas, so there are no other heirs but my grandfather and that young puta he married only a year ago, so—"

"The old goat's married to a hotsy-totsy?" Captain Gringo began to blurt before he caught himself and added, lamely, "Well, we just wouldn't know about your family matters, señora. I wish to Christ someone would tell us why *we* were snatched."

She said she had no idea. After they'd all talked in circles long enough to call one another by their first names, the bully with the earrings came back to tell them that his boss was ready to talk to them now. The girl said she was thirsty. The big Indio told her to see if she could bend her head far enough to suck her own tits. Then he had the two soldiers of fortune dragged out and marched across the camp to a more luxurious canvas tent.

Inside, a smoother but no nicer-looking guy wearing Spanish features, a pimp mustache, and a linen riding outfit was seated at a folding table, eating beans and drinking wine. He told the captives to have a seat, and when they said they didn't see any chairs, he told them they could sit in the mud at his feet. Captain Gringo told him he was all heart but that they preferred to remain standing. So El Jefe had his guards push them down.

As they sat there with their hands tied he said, "That is better. You both appear to be men of common sense. So now you will tell me where my money is, no?"

Captain Gringo tried to look surprised as he replied, "What money are we talking about, and who the fuck are you?"

Their captor looked annoyed and said, "You do not wish to know who I am, señors. There is always an outside chance that you may get out of here alive, if you are very nice to me. So names are not important right now. What is important is that I was to receive a package at the post office in Limón. I did not receive my package. You did. Tell me about it."

Captain Gringo laughed incredulously and said, "So that was what that was all about! Are we talking about a red paper package, addressed to me?"

"We are. Do you deny you signed for it and walked out of the post office with it, Captain Gringo?"

Gaston took a chance. The old con artist said, "Mais non, it was me. Dick, here, was out when a notice about the delivery was shoved under our mutual door at the posada, and as a person in your line of work may be able to understand, a small gray creature like myself attracts less attention in public. They post disgusting pictures in post offices for some reason."

El Jefe snapped, "Never mind which one of you picked it up, damn it. You admit you picked it up. So where is it?"

Gaston shrugged and said, "Quien sabe? Who keeps last week's newspaper? I assumed it was a joke. Then some thugs almost as rude as your own snatched it away from me for some reason. I saw no need to fight for old newspapers. So I did not go into it with them."

El Jefe closed his eyes as if he were making a saintly effort to control himself. But he didn't look at all saintly as he said, "Now listen carefully. I am a man of few words and many bullets. I know all about the dummy package. I sent it. Then I told someone else to send me a package full of money, wrapped in the same red paper.''

"Addressed to *me*, for Pete's sake?" cut in Captain Gringo with an amused sneer. El Jefe did not look amused as he said, "I admit I meant to use you as a ruse. After you picked up the dummy package—and any police watching for whoever picked it up—I meant to have another Captain Gringo pick up the second. I did send a man to pick up the one with the money in it. They told him it had already been picked up. By the person it was addressed to. You. Am I talking too fast for you? Would you like me to speak slower, as my hombres shove a bamboo sliver into the head of your cock and break it inside?"

It wasn't hard to look scared. So Captain Gringo did so as he sighed and said, "It's no use, Gaston. We'd better tell the man the truth, right?"

Gaston shrugged and said, "Oui, he does have a most persuasive manner. Shall I tell him or would you rather?"

Captain Gringo knew Gaston had no idea what he planned to say next. So he said, "I'll come clean, Jefe. We picked up both packages. We didn't know what was in either, of course. We just went separately to the post office, each thinking the other might not, see?"

"I am trying to. Which one of you got the money and for why was it not in your possession when my boys got you?"

"Hell, that's easy. Like Gaston just told you, some other thugs took both packages away from us. How the hell were we supposed to know they were worth fighting over? Neither one of us was expecting a birthday present, you know."

El Jefe shook his head like a bull with a fly between its horns and growled, "Now I am really mixed up. For why are you trying to mix me up? Don't either of you enjoy living?"

Captain Gringo said, "Hey, you think *you're* confused? What about *us*? Some asshole we never heard of sends us mail we couldn't have been expecting. Then some other assholes take it away from us and you expect *us* to explain all this bullshit?"

El Jefe took a deep breath and gave them a breather as he explained what they already really knew from the beginning. When it was his own turn to say something again, Captain Gringo said, "Boy, you sure play chess when the name of the game is checkers, El Jefe. Why the hell did you try such a complicated delivery in the first place? Couldn't you see how many things could go wrong and did? Somebody did have the post office staked, both times. So now somebody else has both deliveries, and don't look at us. By the way, did your guys hurt those girls in our room when they tossed the place?"

"Girls? What girls? Are you trying for to confuse me again?"

"Does anyone have to? You sure have a lot to learn about collecting ransom money, Jefe. You fucked up for sure with those red packages."

El Jefe thought about that as he helped himself to more wine. Then he murmured, "So you say. But there is one very large hole in your story, Captain Gringo. If you two picked up both packages, and I believe you did, how is it that my hombres found you both alive and at large when they ambushed you at the posada? You say the other side had the post office under observation. Bueno. That was what I feared they might try. You say someone then relieved you of both packages. That I find harder to believe. Even you must see that they would have taken you for my men, no?"

Captain Gringo nodded and said, "I guess they must have. So what?"

"So what? Are you trying for to test my self-restraint? What kind of a fool do you take me for? Do you expect me to believe that men lying in wait for someone accepting the delivery of a ransom demand would simply grab the money and let them go?"

Gaston snorted with disgust and said, "Merde alors, this is all too league of the bush to believe. I thought we were discussing business with a professional criminal. Obviously the real crooks got the money and by now must be très amusé, non?''

El Jefe eyed him ominously and said, ''How seriously would you like me to convince you of my criminal intent, you smug little cabron?''

Captain Gringo soothed, ''What he's trying to explain in his own worldly way is that you've been *had*, Jefe. Let's take this apple a bite at a time. If we'd picked up anything staked out by the police, they'd have done it one of only two possible ways. They could have arrested us as kidnappers and tried to make us talk. Or they could have decided to follow us and see if we led them to you. How do you like that so far?''

''Keep talking. I never said you'd been picked up by the police. My instructions were not to contact the police.''

''All right. If the police didn't take both packages and turn us loose, that leaves two gangs who could have, but only *one* who would have let us go. If your kidnap victim's family saw us coming out of that post office with their dinero, do you imagine they'd have just grabbed the money and ran? Why the hell send money in the first place if you want it back *that* bad?''

El Jefe got the pitch. Or the one Captain Gringo had been praying he would. He gasped, ''Madre de Dios! Don Alberto never would have let you go if he thought you were working with me! I see it all now! Some other ladrones found out about the ransom drop and intercepted it! Oh, is there no honesty to be found in this wicked world!''

Captain Gringo shook his head and said, ''Not much. Can we go home now?''

The outlaw leader looked startled and replied, ''I wish you would not make idle jests when I am trying for to think. For why should I set you free, even if I believed you?''

Captain Gringo answered, ''Well, nobody's about to ransom us, and if you're thinking about recruiting us to help you get the money, forget it. Gaston's right. You guys don't know your business, and we don't work with amateurs.''

''Who said anything about recruiting you, for the love of

God? The thought had not even crossed my mind, I assure you!''

Captain Gringo and Gaston exchanged knowing glances. The little Frenchman murmured, ''See? What did I tell you?''

El Jefe frowned down at them and declared, ''As a matter of fact, I was pondering the best way to dispose of possible witnesses.'' So Captain Gringo nodded soberly and said, ''When you're right, you're right, Gaston. The guy's afraid that two wanted men are anxious to march into a police station and say naughty things about him. We don't know who he is, or shit about the case, but I guess some guys worry a lot. Thank God he gets to worry about recovering the money from that other gang. It figures to be a bitch, now that he's fucked it all up.''

El Jefe rose, walked around the table, and kicked Captain Gringo flat before he asked soberly, ''I would like to hear just how you would go about recovering my dinero, if you are so smart.''

Captain Gringo stayed down as he replied in a desperately casual tone, ''I'm not sure I could, this late in the game. Like I said, you fucked it up with all that red-paper razzle-dazzle. The girl's people think they paid the ransom. So you'll pay hell getting them to send you another centavo now.''

''Oh, I don't know. Suppose I sent them her ear, or perhaps a nipple or two to persuade them?''

''That would persuade them that what they'll already be sweating bullets over must be true, of course. They paid the ransom. You didn't send her back alive. So about now they'll be giving her up for dead in any case, and who's going to pay for parts of a corpse?''

''All right. What do you suggest I do to persuade them?''

''I just said I don't see how, God damn it. They have you down as a double-crosser. If they don't see the girl alive, poco tiempo, now that they've paid off, they'll be going to the police any minute and things will get even more complicated. The only way you'll get that money will be by taking it back from whoever has it right now, and don't look at us. You know damn well *we* don't have it.''

''Bueno. So who does?''

''How the fuck should I know? I just told you they grabbed it and ran. If we'd been in on it with them . . . Oh, shit, do we have to keep talking in circles?''

''Si, we have to keep talking until I discover where my money is.''

Captain Gringo sat back up and said, ''Okay, have your apes untie us, and let's put our heads together.''

''Can you not talk from down there, amigo?''

''Sure, I can talk all you like. But what can I tell you? The only way we can get the money back calls for figuring out who the hell *has* it! By the way, what's our share if we help you get it back?''

''Share? What share are you talking about? You two are not members of this organization!''

''No? Well, we'd better be, if we're going to help you find out who those other crooks are and help you fight 'em. I doubt like hell that they'll hand over that much dinero without a fight. How much money of ours are they holding, by the way?''

El Jefe started to answer. Then a look of low cunning crossed his face as he replied, ''Two thousand, American. That is a lot of money in this part of the world.''

So Captain Gringo did his best not to sigh with relief. He knew they'd have to go through some more of this bullshit. But if El Jefe wasn't planning to enlist them and double-cross them, he wouldn't have lied about the money, right?

It felt good to be up and around with those itchy ropes off, but they weren't out of the woods yet. El Jefe had told them not to be silly when they asked for their guns back and told his segundo to keep an eye on them while he checked out a

couple of ideas they'd suggested. So the big Indio kept
following them around like a dog as they tried to act relaxed.
It was apparently all right to help themselves to coffee and
beans at the communal campfire. But Gaston said he found it
très fatigué that a man could not even take a piss in private
these days. It was later than Captain Gringo had thought, no
doubt in more ways than one. So the sun was low in what
they now knew was the west and, with luck, nobody could
get back to Limón and back before morning to louse up the
bill of goods they'd semi-sold the suspicious El Jefe. He
seemed to be sulking in his tent while he waited to hear more
about some nonexistent rogues Gaston had advised him to
question first. The only bright spot, so far, was that they
could assume that the gang had no sneaks in Don Alberto's
camp. Their razzle-dazzle wouldn't have worked if, as Teresa
suspected, her kidnapping had been an inside job.

They didn't tell her that. They didn't go anywhere near the
pretty captive once they'd been given limited freedom of the
outlaw camp. El Jefe was still muttering darkly about ears in
pickle jars, and they didn't want to remind him that she was
still around.

As the sun set the big Indio showed them a lean-to not far
from the more elaborate hut the girl was being held in, and
told them they could bed down there. When Gaston asked
about bedding, the segundo suggested that they snuggle up to
keep warm and wandered off, muttering about all whites
being sissies.

Gaston sat cross-legged on the leaves someone had shov-
eled under the overhang and lit a smoke, muttering, "Sacré
God damn, the least they could offer us would be some
adelitas, non?"

Captain Gringo hunkered down beside him as he observed,
"I don't think they have enough adelitas to go around. I size
this bunch up as part-time banditos. Probably city boys at
heart. If they were far from home, they'd have more horses as
well as more dames. The newspaper stuffed in that dummy
package was a local Limón edition, remember?"

"Oui, El Jefe strikes me as a pimp too. The girl is supposed to remember them as a jungle band. Ergo, they *did* mean to let her go in the end, non?"

"I'm not too sure El Jefe knows *what* the fuck he's doing. He has to be a small-town crook with big-time notions. Those are the kinds you have to worry about. When do you think we'd better make our break for it, this side of moonrise or the other?"

Gaston sighed **and** said, "I wish you would not say things like that, Dick. Both sound très dangereux. If we run for it by the light of the silvery moon, we are sure to catch some lead with our adorable derrieres. If we run for it in the dark, we are sure to be eaten by crocodiles. We don't even know which way to run, and the night-feeding creepy crawlies are everywhere in the dark, hein?"

"Yeah. I guess we'd better wait for the moon. I think we're northwest of Limón. I wouldn't want to look for it in total darkness."

"Neither would I. That brings us back to the subject of people with guns, which we seem to lack for some reason. Running gunfights by moonlight are bad enough. I never indulge in them unarmed!"

Captain Gringo got out his next-to-last claro and lit up before he insisted, "You'd better, unless you want to wait here until those guys El Jefe sent into town come back to tell him we could be fibbing. I don't know where our guns are now, and I hope El Jefe's got some wine, women, or whatever, to keep him busy for the next few hours. But how many times can we hope to bullshit him?"

"I didn't think it would work the last time. Eh bien, here is my plan. We abscond as soon as it is dark enough. Then we hole up, well off in the spinache, to await the rising of the moon. If we can find some trail, other than the ones these unwashed types will surely cover, there is only a fifty-fifty chance we'll be going down it the wrong way. Even getting lost in the jungle has to be safer than being here when El Jefe starts pouting again, hein?"

Captain Gringo nodded and said, "Okay. I'd better alert Teresa that we'll be leaving soon."

But as he started to rise Gaston grabbed him and hissed, "Are you out of your adorable mind, Dick? We can't risk taking a soft, spoiled Spanish girl with us!"

Captain Gringo frowned and replied, "We can't risk leaving her here, either, damn it. That fucking El Jefe was talking about cutting her nipples off *before* we got him really pissed!"

"True. But while we may be risking her life if we leave her here, we are sure to get all three of us killed if we try to carry her with us. Our only chance calls for moving tout de suite and far, long before we are missed. They check their more valuable prisoner often. We could not hope to get an hour's lead on them if we tried to take her along."

Captain Gringo shook his head and said, "Okay, so we get to run like hell for an hour. We'll watch her doorway and sneak her out right after they check her ropes. Come on. Let's let her in on the plan before she tries to go to sleep. She's going to have to be wide-awake, indeed, if she hopes to move worth a damn right after we untie her."

Gaston followed Captain Gringo to his feet, muttering under his breath as the taller American moved toward Teresa's hut in the gathering darkness. Not wanted to be spotted from the campfire, and knowing how flimsy the thatched walls were, Captain Gringo moved in along the line of trees to enter by the back door he meant to tear open. So, inside the hut, the segundo had no way of guessing that he was being overheard as he told the struggling captive, "Be nice, querida. For why do you keep trying to kick me in the cajones, eh? You know you want it. All women want it. It is the nature of the beasts."

Teresa was trying to scream and not having much luck with the big Indio's palm clamped over her mouth like that. So when Captain Gringo burst through the thatch and landed on the segundo like a ton of pissed-off bricks, the Indio naturally let go of her face, and she screamed loud enough to wake the dead. Or, at any rate, any dead less dead than the segundo crushed under Captain Gringo's enraged and still-hitting weight. Gaston grabbed the big Yank from behind and hissed, "Enough! Can't you see he's spilled his bladder and bowels, Dick? How many times do you have to break the same spine and . . . will you please shut up, señora?"

She did, once she figured out what was going on. But as Captain Gringo rolled the dead bandito away from her and proceeded to take off his gun rig, a voice from outside called, "Hey, Indio. You need help in there? I like cherry, too, hombre!"

Neither soldier of fortune had an answer for that. But Teresa turned out to be a fast thinker when she wasn't screaming. Her voice was low and dirty as she called back, "Go away, muchacho. Cannot a lady have some privacy around here?"

"Oh, you Indio!" laughed the other outlaw, turning away with a very lewd suggestion indeed. Captain Gringo handed one of the dead man's guns to Gaston, stuck the other in the waistband of his own pants, and started to untie the girl as he whispered, "Nice going. That ought to give us an even better lead. Who checks prisoners when they know they're being, ah, watched?"

"He tried for to rape me, Dick." She sobbed. So he said, "We noticed. Don't blubber up on us again, God damn it! Here, I'll help you up. We have to get out of here now!"

"Pero, Dick, I have no shoes! They took my shoes away! I don't think I can run barefoot through the jungle!"

"Sure you can. First you lift your right foot, then your left. Or would you rather stay here and wait to see who shows up for sloppy seconds?"

"Must you be so brutal, damn you?"

"Brutal or frutal, we're leaving. Gaston, grab her ankles and take the lead. Let's go."

Gaston didn't argue. He only talked too much when it didn't matter. He picked up Teresa's bare ankles and bulled out the back way as Captain Gringo carried the rest of her and the ammo belts. Carrying her that way wasn't bad for the first quarter of a mile. Then Gaston stopped, swore, and said, "End of the line. We seem to have run into a très large body of water."

Captain Gringo sat Teresa on a fallen log and moved around to morosely survey the sorry situation. The moon wasn't up yet. But even by starlight one could see the broad expanse of still water ahead. He muttered, "Maybe if we wade it, sort of slow and easy . . ." But then a fish jumped and something even bigger jumped after it to catch it in midair. So he didn't answer as Gaston remarked, "You were saying . . . ?"

Teresa sobbed, "My God, we're trapped," and both soldiers of fortune wondered what else was new. Looking back the way they'd just come, they could still see the campfire glow through the tree boles. Captain Gringo started to ask her if she had any idea where Limón might be. Then he remembered that she'd been carried here unconscious and thought it more sensible to suggest, "We work our way along the edge to the north. That trail we came in by runs to the south."

Gaston said, "True. Mais, won't that mean we are probably going even deeper into the spinache, Dick?"

"Right now we can't get too deep in it to suit me! The trail could loop all over hell. We know that they know we know it's the only trail out of this neck of the woods. So that's what they'll try first. Let's go. I'm sorry, honey. But you have to start walking. We're running out of time."

She stood up, took a step, and winced, saying, "I'll try. But I don't know how far I can walk like this."

"Hell, look on the bright side, kid. At the rate we're going how far can we get before they catch us?"

As it turned out, it wasn't far. The moon was beginning to pearl the sinister water to their right when, ahead, they spotted more of the same. Another damned jungle stream, a wide one, entered the one barring progress to the east at right angles from the west, to bar further progress to the north. Captain Gringo chewed the end of his unlit cigar as he considered this. He was already pissed enough when Gaston asked, "Eh bien, know any other interesting shortcuts?"

"Look, maybe if we can work upstream, around the north end of the camp..."

"To where, sacré God damn? Is it not obvious that our adorable El Jefe sited his disgusting jungle camp with a view to entrances and exits? It sits at the end of that gun runner's trail to nowhere, guarded on at least two sides by open water, so..."

"So if the dog hadn't stopped to sniff it's mama, it might have whatever. Let's go. We sure as hell can't stay here. Any minute, admiration for the segundo's staying power has to turn to wonder, and you can almost see the damned camp from here!"

Gaston took the lead. The jungle floor this close to water was squishy soft. But Teresa still bitched every time she stepped on a twig. Gaston sat down on another fallen tree and proceeded to take off his mosquito boots, muttering, "I feel sure your feet are bigger than mine, you spoiled species of cow, mais we shall have to do something about your constant mooing!"

It might have worked. They might even have skirted the camp to the north before it came unstuck. But they would never know. For just then, all hell broke loose.

Captain Gringo grabbed the girl and flattened behind Gaston's log with her as a bullet wanged into it from the other side. Gaston leapt off it as yet another round blew punky splinters from the place he'd just been sitting. More bullets were thudding into more wood above them as the little Frenchman got his stolen gun out and gasped, "Sacré God damn, could all that be meant for little old me?"

Captain Gringo growled, "Hold your fire. Those are stray rounds flying out of camp. Let's not tell anyone there's a target out here. Make 'em guess!"

They did as the fusillade continued, and they tried to figure out what was going on. As they heard the death rattle of automatic fire Captain Gringo gasped, "I don't remember seeing a machine gun in that camp! Did either of you?"

Gaston said, "Mais non! Yet there it goes again and you are right. It is a machine gun, firing in deadly earnest at someone I feel glad I am not keeping company with at the moment!"

The mysterious machine gun began another burst, then stopped in mid-sentence. Captain Gringo observed, "Looks like they got him, if his gun didn't just jam."

"Oui, but someone seems to be making up for the silence with small arms fire! What could all that noise mean, Dick?"

"Shut up and listen," Captain Gringo suggested. So they did, and after a while the firefight faded away to occasional single shots. Gaston nodded from experience and said, "They're taking care of the wounded now. I wonder who won. That was too much shooting to have been an internal squabble, hein?"

"No question about that. The gang got jumped by some-body! Teresa, does your grandfather own a machine gun?"

She said, "He could. I told you he was very rich."

He nodded, still undecided. Then he saw that the question was academic. Outlined by the orange glow in the distance, a skirmish line of guys in uniform were headed their way, and there was no place to go. So he got rid of his stolen revolver and stood up, hands high, to call out, "Don't shoot! We're on your side, I hope!"

The advancing riflemen didn't shoot, but they didn't treat anyone too nicely as they marched them back into camp, or what was left of it. Dead bodies lay sprawled all over the campsite. El Jefe's tent was down, and so was El Jefe, judging by the way someone wearing his boots had soaked the folds of canvas draped across that man-sized lump. The machine gun they'd heard was set up on its tripod by the fire. It was a Maxim. Who the quasi-uniformed bozo standing by it with a quizzical smile might be was still up for grabs.

One of the men who'd rounded up the soldiers of fortune and the girl called out, "We found these out in the trees,

Generale. They say they are on our side. I did not know
anyone else *was* on our side, but I thought you might wish for
to speak to them before we shot them, eh?"

El Generale waved the captives in politely enough and
suggested that they explain what they might be.

Captain Gringo pointed at the body under the wrecked tent
and said, "These hombres were holding us prisoner. I take it
you must be the Costa Rican Guard?"

El Generale snorted in disgust and asked, "Do I look like a
sissy? Do you not recognize the uniform of Nicaragua when
you see it, you tourist?"

Captain Gringo managed not to gulp before he replied, as
lightly as he could, "Oh, come to think of it, you do look
like Nicaraguan regulars, sort of. I guess we just weren't
expecting to meet up with your army this far south of the
border, Generale."

The man in the quasi-uniform made up of bits and pieces
stolen from at least three armies shrugged and said, "Those
are the fortunes of war. El Tio Sam, for some reason, seems
to favor the enemies of the Nicaraguan people. By the way, I
mean no disrespect, but is that not a Yanqui accent you are
wearing, señor, ah . . . ?"

"Walker, Ricardo Walker, and this is Gaston Verrier. You
may recall us fighting for your side the last time we were up
your way, sir!"

That was true, no matter which side was winning this
season, as the two of them had fought on *both* sides in the
ongoing, Nicaraguan civil war.

El General muttered, "Walker? Walker? The only Yanqui
named Walker I recall was a would-be dictator who got shot
trying for to meddle in Nicaraguan political matters, and you
are too young to be him even if he was . . . oh, muchacho
mio! You are not by any chance the Walker they call Captain
Gringo?"

The slightly older man sounded happy about it. So Captain
Gringo flipped the coin their lives were embossed on and
nodded modestly. El Generale grabbed him like a long-lost

son and bear-hugged him as he blew garlic and pepper in his
ear, explaining, "We could not have met at a better time,
Captain Gringo! The pobrecito I'd issued our only automatic
weapon to was killed only minutes ago! You are just what I
need right now! I have heard of your brave compañero,
Gaston, and this is your adelita, eh? I must say you know
how to pick them, you dog. She is muy linda. How are you
called, my pretty muchacha?"

The Spanish girl was fortunately too scared to say more
than, "I am called Teresa, señor."

"Bueno. You must have run off from a good family.
Anyone can see you have Spanish blood." Said the guerrilla
leader, letting go of Captain Gringo to shout, "Attend me,
you unwashed scum of the earth and the even dirtier whores
they sleep with! These new recruits are Captain Gringo and
his adelita Teresa, the ugly little man is the Great Gaston
you may have heard of, so do not try for to fuck *him*, either!"

Someone shouted, "Viva Captain Gringo." Someone usually did. El Generale smiled approvingly and turned back to
his "recruits" to ask, "Tell me, Captain Gringo, who were
these idiots we just wiped out?"

"They were bandits, Generale. Their leader was only
called El Jefe. We know little about them, since they just
captured us."

"Ah, no doubt they intended to turn you in for the prices
on your heads, no? Bueno, you are safe with us now."

Teresa asked, "Why did you shoot all these people if you
did not know who they were?" Some dames just had to ask.
Gaston kicked her bare ankle to shut her up as El Generale
shrugged and replied matter-of-factly, "They had guns, food,
ammunition. We needed all three. We have a long way to go,
in hostile country, my children."

"We're going somewhere?" asked Captain Gringo mildly.
So El Generale announced, "Si, back to free our country. We
were driven over the border far to the west but now we have
more ammunition, and those ladrones will never expect us to
return from this far east. I may have forgotten to tell you. I

am Generale Verdugo, a well-known military genius. I am always surprising people.''

Captain Gringo agreed that was for sure, as Gaston grabbed Teresa by one wrist and tried to inform her by mental telepathy that if even one of these guys discovered that she was worth real money, they'd *really* be in trouble!

Teresa didn't spill the beans that night. Captain Gringo didn't let her. For fastidious reasons, El Generale decided to make camp a mile away, since that was less work than cleaning up his most recent massacre. By the time some lesser guerrillas had thrown together a hut for the great Captain Gringo and his adelita, Teresa had found some shoes and some of her native wit. But she still started talking dumb again as soon as she was alone in a hut, with one bedroll, with Captain Gringo. She gasped. ''I can't spend the night with you, Dick! I am not that kind of woman!''

He said, ''You don't even get three guesses what kind of woman you'll wind up if these guerrillas don't think you're with me. Don't be so egotistical. Did I say I wanted to lay you? The last guy who tried that got kneed in the cajones, if I recall his last words correctly.''

She laughed despite herself and said, ''I know I owe you for that, Dick. But women of my class do not repay the knight who saves them from the dragon in such peasant fashions as you may be used to. Why can't we simply tell this strange generale the truth? He seems like a reasonable man, no?''

''No. You were closer to the mark when you called him strange. He's either fighting sincerely for the long-lost cause to the north, or, more than likely, he's just another bush bandit using the trouble up that way as an excuse. He swatted El Jefe like a fly, without bothering to ask his political views. Either way, he needs money, and you, my frigid dear, are money on the hoof. So we don't want to tell him where he might lay his hands on an easy ten grand. That's more than our General Washington started out with!''

She sank to her knees on the bedding but asked, ''How do you mean to get me out of here, then?''

He said, ''Not tonight, Josephine. We've had enough running for one night. Our best bet is to go along with the gag until we wind up somewhere a little more civilized. Unlike that first bunch, this bunch won't be expecting us to make a break for it. I'm a known soldier of fortune, and they don't know how sneaky I can get. We'll get you home. Just don't push it. It's dumb to take chances before you know you have a chance, see?''

She reclined on one elbow and replied, ''I think so. But how are we to go on pretending I am your . . . What is an adelita, Dick?''

''About what it sounds like. A fancy word for a camp follower. The real Adelita is a girl in an old Spanish marching song. The mujeres prefer the title to ruder ones, see?''

''It does sound much nicer than puta. Are all those other girls out there, ah, you-know-whats?''

''Some may be married to their soldados. These guerrilla bands are sort of informal about legal niceties, as El Jefe just found out. Don't act snotty with any of the other adelitas and you won't have any trouble with 'em. Most of them are just simple peon girls who mean well. Real whores would be too smart to follow a guy around until he wound up dead.''

''You are right. They must be stupid. But if I am to pass for one, you will have to show me how, no?''

He lay down beside her and said, ''Well, come morning we'll have to see about more sensible clothes. You look more like a wayward debutante than a military volunteer in that outfit, and some peon girls are likely to be jealous of real silk, even torn and dirty. Let me worry about it. You've had a hard day, kid. Try to catch some sleep.''

''In this bedroll, with a strange man?''

''I'm not so strange. Can we knock off the prick teasing

now? I said to get some sleep, not to open wide and say 'ah,' God damn it!''

Her eyes blazed. She started to slap him, thought better of it, and sobbed. "Oh, how could you speak to me like that? I am not used to being treated like this, you brute!"

He grinned crookedly down at her and replied, "You're going to have to get used to it unless you start talking sense, Teresa. I don't admire prick teasers, and I'm the closest thing to a gentleman you'll be talking to until we can get you out of here, see?"

"Oh, you said it again! How dare you mention the private parts of a man in the company of a lady?"

"I didn't bring the subject up. You did. I'll never understand dames like you. You bust a gut looking yummy, bat your eyes, and talk about sex, and then you go all shy-convent-girl when a man even looks at you."

She shook her head wildly, tossing her black curls becomingly, as she protested, "That is not true. It was you, just now, who suggested that we sleep together!"

He shook his own head and said, "Suggested it, hell. We don't have any choice. The others outside would wonder a lot about a soldado who didn't want to sleep with his own adelita. So aside from my being taken for a sissy, you could find yourself fending off another sudden admirer. What happened in that other camp was partly your fault, you know."

She gasped and demanded, "Are you suggesting that I encouraged the advances of that ruffian you saved me from?"

So he said, "He was only the segundo. I don't imagine El Jefe gave him orders to rape you. So he must have thought it was okay by you until you kicked him in the nuts. Look, *I* know you didn't think you were flirting with that Indio. But *he* did. You have natural bedroom eyes and a dumb way of talking to men. We can't do much about the eyes. If you don't want men leaping on your bones, don't bring the subject up. Some guys ain't as couth as me. So they naturally figure a dame who brings the subject up must be interested in the subject."

"Listen here, it was you, not I, who mentioned going to bed with me, you brute!"

"No, *you* listen, you silly broad. I told you to get some sleep. I didn't even ask you to kiss me night-night. So what gave you the right to assume that I had mad carnal desires for you?"

She lowered her lashes and tried to suppress a smile. The results were Mona Lisa as she asked, "Well, don't you? Most men seem to want me, for some reason."

He laughed despite himself and said, "That's neither here nor there. The point is that I've yet to make a pass at you, and frankly, I'm a little hurt that you dames seem to take me so for granted. Just move over some and pull the covers over you and we'll say no more about it, right? I promise not to ravage you like the beast I am while I have you in my wicked power and all that shit."

Teresa lay flat and pulled the canvas as high as her semi-exposed chest as she said with sad resignation, "Easy for you to say now. But you forget that I have been married, Dick. You men are all alike in the stillness of the night."

She probably had a point. She sure was built, even in dim light and under stiff canvas. It was too early for a guy with a dawning erection to consider sleeping innocently. So even though he knew it was smarter to lay low in strange surroundings at first, he crawled out of the hut and stood up to see what else was going on.

Nothing much was, outside the huts. From the passionate moans coming through some of the improvised walls he passed, some other camp followers couldn't be so shy. He moved toward the central fire. There was nobody in sight but a sad-looking adelita sitting cross-legged by the canvas-draped machine gun. Captain Gringo hunkered down to remove the night cloth as he asked the girl if there was any coffee left. She sighed and said, "The cook is off-duty. Please do not beat me if you find that weapon dirty, Captain Gringo. I do my best. But in God's truth it is difficult keeping metal rust-free in this climate without proper cleaning materials."

He said he'd noticed that as he opened the action of the
Maxim machine gun and found it had been cleaned and oiled
since the last time it had been fired. The head spacing was set
right too. He nodded and told her, "This gun would pass
inspection most anywhere. But how come you say you
cleaned it? El Generale told me you just lost your only heavy
weapons man, señorita . . . ?"

"I am called Ernesta. As you see, I am not a man. The
gunner I was assigned to assist is the person you are speaking
of."

He stared thoughtfully. She was right about being a woman, and a damned pretty one if a guy admired tawny mestiza
types. He said, "I am sorry you lost your hombre. I must say
that he trained you well as his loader."

Ernesta wrinkled her pert nose and replied, "He was not
my hombre, and it was I who taught him. My late husband
was Regular Army, killed two years ago fighting on the
Granada side up north. It was from him I learned how to man
and care for a machine gun. Our garrison was small, and
everyone there had to know for how to defend the post."

He cut in to assure her that he knew the Granada troops
were swell eggs and asked her how come she'd wound up
way down here with a guerilla band.

She sighed and said, "Our post was overwhelmed. I was
not shot with the men and ugly women because I was not
ugly. Later I managed to knife the soldado they gave me to
and make my escape. I fell in with El Generale, who is not a
bad man, even if he is a bit stupid. When he learned that I
knew about machine guns, he ordered me to load for his
machine gunner. The one who was killed tonight. Now *there*
was a really stupid man. Do you know how he managed to
get picked off, even as we were winning?"

Captain Gringo nodded and said, "Sure. He was firing
long bursts from one position. Somebody fired up his muzzle
flashes."

Ernesta looked even prettier when she smiled and said,
"Oh, you *do* know how it is done. I warned him that it was

time for to shift the tripod. He did not listen to me. Nobody listens to a woman at such times.''

Captain Gringo said, "I'll listen, if you still want to act as loader. Would you rather be somewhere else, Ernesta?"

She shrugged and replied, "I have no place else to be now. The Leon Faction now controls the part of Nicaragua I am from, and as I just told you, I have no man back there in any case."

He nodded understandingly and said, "Bueno. In that case, should anyone ask, you are my loader and, if you need protection, you can say you're my adelita as well."

She stared up at him thoughtfully, then said, "I saw the adelita you already have. She is very beautiful. Do you think I would make a convincing adelita for the Great Captain Gringo?"

"Sure, I'm supposed to be horny as hell, and I guess my rank calls for at least two adelitas. Don't think I'm getting fresh with you. I know you just lost your, ah, machine gunner, so . . ."

"He was not my lover, damn it!" She blazed, adding, "He wanted to be. But I do not make love with men I have no respect for, and as I said, he was very stupid and a most poor soldado."

He got back to his feet and said, "Look, you can work it out any way you like. Just tell me what you tell the others, and I'll back you. If you want to be my loader, I can use a loader. If you'd rather say you were someone else's adelita, that's no problem."

She rose, too, to answer, "I wish for to be your loader, and I wish for to say I am your adelita segunda. You know how some men treat a woman with no protector."

"We were just talking about that in my hut. By the way, where are you supposed to be sleeping right now?"

She pointed across the campfire and replied, "I built my shelter over that way. I could not sleep because I had much on my mind. So I came out here to make sure the Maxim was well covered. But you are right. It is getting late, and El

Generale is a fiend for marching. Would you care to sleep with me or your other adelita this night, Captain Gringo?''

He gulped and said, ''Under the circumstances you can call me Dick. You know any man would want to sleep with you, of course. But are you sure you want me to?''

She shrugged and replied, ''I do not know yet. But if I am to be your adelita segunda, don't you think we should find out?''

They did. The pragmatic little peon led him to her little shack, and they just got in her bedroll together, as if they'd been shacked up for some time. He was sure she was just cleaning up her past a bit by claiming not to have had a man for some time, until he mounted her warm, hungry flesh and learned how hungry it was. But as she began to move under him with the skill of a very experienced woman indeed, he began to wonder if his first idea might not have been right. It was a lot of fun making up his mind, and Ernesta said she liked the way he moved in her too. She said it matter-of-factly, with no mush or fake passion. So he couldn't help feeling flattered when she began to show real passion once the ice was broken. Her orgasm was almost painful, to him at least. For the muscular peon girl was well legged-up from marching under heavy loads, and he might have found the way she gripped him with her strong brown thighs uncomfortable if he hadn't been ejaculating in her tight, warm little love maw so enjoyably.

As they shared an after-pleasure smoke together Ernesta asked, ''Did you find that tolerable, Captain Gringo? I warned you that I was out of practice, but I tried to please you.''

He snuggled her head closer on his bare shoulder and told her, ''I told you to call me Dick, and it wasn't tolerable, it was grand. No offense, but you sure screw good, querida.''

''Es verdad? I am glad. You are much man, and you almost drove me out of my mind with pleasure just now. Could we do it one more time before you must return to my superior adelita?''

He laughed and said, "I'll be the judge of who's superior. Just let me get my second wind."

"Oh, you wish for to make love to me a second time in one night? I feel honored as well as most warm between my legs now. I so hoped you would enjoy my body. But I was afraid you would not think me as good for to fuck as that prettier blanca of yours. Are you sure she will not mind if her segunda has you twice in a row?"

He offered her a drag on his claro as he told her, "Naw, old Teresa's a good sport. I don't want you two arguing over me. Is that understood?"

"Si, I know she has first claim on you. I know my place. I do not pick fights with other women. It is up to the man to decide with whom he wishes to rut, no?"

"Close enough. I sure admire old-fashioned girls like you. But as long as we're discussing ground rules, fess up. Were you or were you not hanging around my machine gun in hopes that something like this might happen?"

She started to deny it. Then she gave an embarrassed little giggle and confessed, "In God's truth, the results were even more than I was hoping for. I was so afraid you would not want me, even for your loader, and *then* what would have become of me?"

He didn't answer. They both knew the answer, and he found the practical side of being a woman a little disturbing. Down deep inside he knew that the difference between a lady insisting on a ring and a puta insisting on enough for her next warm meal could be dismissed by a cynic as a matter of comparative price. But he liked women too much to feel cynical about them. So he wished they wouldn't *be* so goddamn practical about romantic matters.

Ernesta didn't understand his silence. So she reached down to take a practical approach to life and, as she stroked him, asked him just when he had to get back to Teresa. He said, "Hold the thought. You're holding it just fine right now. I told you there was no hurry. We've got all night. Or most of it, anyway. I suppose I ought to pop out of that other hut in the morning. Don't want to make El Generale nervous.''

Ernesta sat up to get a better grip on the situation as she said with a pleased expression, ''You should have told me she was having her period. I am so glad. I mean her no disrespect, but may I assume you have not been in her, ah, recently?''

He closed his eyes and lay back to enjoy what she was doing down there as he assured her, ''Oh, I haven't been in another woman in ages.'' So Ernesta said, ''Bueno!'' and dived on his dawning erection headfirst. He hissed in pure animal pleasure as she went to work with her wet, pursed lips. She sure knew how to French, and he didn't want to know where she'd learned. But just in case she was fibbing about that other machine gunner, he was reluctant to return the favor with his own mouth. So he snuffed out the cigar and began to play her clit by hand in hopes that it would be enough for her.

It apparently was. Ernesta began to suck wildly as he strummed her old banjo while she got above him with a knee planted to either side of his rib cage. He put his other hand in her to massage her cervix with questing fingertips as he played with her engorged little man in the boat. He could tell by the resultant contractions that she was about to climax that way, and since she obviously *wanted* to climax that way, he let her, as she sucked him off all the way.

Then he rolled her limp, quivering form off him to swap ends and get back in her right. As he entered her still-pulsing orgasmic vagina Ernesta crooned, ''Is this possible? Is there yet more to come?'' So he kissed her warmly and replied, ''Yeah, let's come some more.''

''I shall, I shall, I *am,* and oh, querido, I am so happy! Would you mind very much if I told you I loved you, just a little? I know it is a foolish thing to say. But I feel like saying it and saying it as you fuck me over and over and over!''

He assured her that he didn't mind a little mush, as long as she didn't overdo it. So she kept sobbing how much she loved him as he had her old-fashioned, doggie-style, and with her on top when it began to fade from true lust to just showing off. Later she assured him that she would never tell his other adelita that she loved him or, God forbid, that she'd blown him all the way. He didn't ask her to take it anywhere else. He felt sure she would, but the bathing facilities around here were a little limited and, what the hell, sodomy was uncalled for when a gal was built so tight all over.

He let her fall asleep in his arms. It was easy enough for her after all the work she'd done under and on top of him. Then he eased her head off his shoulder and slipped his duds back on. As he crept out of her hut he saw that the campfire had died down to faintly glowing embers and that nothing was stirring in the ruby light. So he was a bit surprised as, heading back to the other hut, he heard Gaston call out cheerfully, "Eh bien. I was hoping you did not mean to spend the whole night with that mestiza."

"You peeked?" Asked Captain Gringo as the Frenchman joined him in the privacy of open space. Gaston handed Captain Gringo back his old shoulder rig and said, "Mais non, there was no need to peek when these ears of the fox detected a woman sobbing that she was possibly wounded très fatale by a cock of astounding proportions. What was the matter with the Spanish girl, crabs or the clap? If you don't want her, let your elders show you how to treat a lady. I am immune to the clap and know how to deal with crabs."

Captain Gringo removed his jacket to strap his .38 back on as he growled, "Never mind about the dames. Where did you get our guns?"

"From the other camp, of course. I did not have two females in heat distracting me. I thought they might have been keeping our stolen gear in El Jefe's tent. They were, after some searching. I found something better as I pawed around over there. I found a map. This jungle must have made the late El Jefe nervous too. I thought he was a city boy. Eh bien, we are perhaps thirty kilometers northwest of

Limón. If we started running now, we could make it just after dawn, non?''

"Non. It's later than that, and I'm not up to running anywhere right now for some reason. Teresa will be lucky if she can walk, even after a good night's sleep. Hide the map away and try to keep track of where we are. Our best bet would be a shorter run to someplace closer, where they have lots and lots of cops. El Generale has a big gang, a machine gun, and an uncertain temper.''

He filled Gaston in on what Ernesta had told him, leaving out the naughty parts, as Gaston walked him the rest of the way to the hut he was supposed to be sharing with Teresa. He promised Gaston that he'd ask Ernesta if she had a friend who admired older men and ducked inside to see how Teresa was making out.

She wasn't making out so hot. She was still awake and, for some reason, crying again. He stretched out beside her, atop the covers, and asked, "Now what's wrong, for God's sake?''

She replied, "I was afraid you and Gaston had run off without me and that I would be raped any minute by these terrible bandits!''

He shucked everything but his shirt and pants as he told her, "Let's get out of the habit of calling El Generale a bandit. I'm sure he feels he's a guerrilla.''

"There is a difference?''

"Not really, but it's safer to be polite. A bandit is a guy who just runs around robbing people. A guerrilla is a guy who says he has an excuse. It's considered sort of noble for Nicaraguans to rob Nicaraguans in the name of Nicaragua, just like Irish rebels rob Irishmen for Irish freedom or the late Jesse James robbed southerners in the name of the Confederacy.''

"But, Dick, we are not in Nicaragua now. How can El Generale rob Costa Ricans in the name of Nicaraguan anything?''

"Easy. He's got lots of guns. I just got his version of Robin Hood. His bunch was chased down here by a bigger gang of thugs in the name of Nicaraguan freedom. He'd made an end run and hopes to get back up north to free some more Nicaraguan pigs and chickens. So let's not discourage the notion, okay?''

''But I do not wish for to go to Nicaragua, Dick! You must help me get back to my grandfather and my people at once!''

Captain Gringo warned her, ''Keep it down. Adelitas don't give orders. I've been thinking about the best way to get you back to Don Alberto. I think you'd both like it better if we got you back alive. So aside from near and present dangers, we'd better bone up on our options. That other gang were city slickers, and you said you might have been drugged in your own home. Run that stuff about your wicked step-grandmother past me again. We wouldn't want to dash madly at a light burning in the window only for you to find it was a gun muzzle, see?''

''Oh, you agree my poor grandfather married a common slut?''

''I don't know anything about her. She could be a swell kid who just admires older men, or a lady who wants it all when he kicks the bucket. Frankly I can't see even a wicked step-grandmother having you snatched when there are so many less complicated ways to get rid of unwanted heirs. Snow White's stepmother told the hunter to kill her, not to hold her for ransom, remember?''

''Who is this Snow White of yours, Dick?''

''Never mind. Tell me about the wicked whatever who married Don Alberto lately.''

Teresa curled a pretty lip and sneered. ''She is, as I said, a pig. A stupid slut who puts horns on my poor grandfather every chance she gets, and she gets many chances, since my grandfather goes to bed at sundown. I have seen her myself, cruising the plaza during the hours of paseo, trying to pick up men.''

''What were *you* trying to pick up at the paseo, women?''

''It is not the same. I am a widow, and in any case, I only go there once in a while for to look. My poor grandfather's wife goes out while he is sleeping for to be truly wicked and . . . Oh, Dick, I just thought of something! That Indio, the one you saved me from, I think I saw him one night in town, flirting with that dirty little bitch who married my grandfather for his money!''

"Are you sure? Lots of guys with Indian features wear earrings.''

Teresa frowned thoughtfully and said, "I am almost certain now that it was him. He was not dressed so roughly, of course. He had on a white suit such as Anglo tourists wear and, no, he was not wearing earrings. But he said while he was trying for to rape me that he knew me and—''

"Right,'' Captain Gringo cut in, "we know that at least some of the kidnappers had to be city slickers, and it does look as if you were set up by someone in town. Let's put the Indio on the back burner for now and get back to the lady you *know* you don't like. How is she called?''

"Her name is Melina. I am sure she bleaches her hair, the pig.''

Captain Gringo coughed on his claro, cleared his throat, and softly said, "So am I. Are we talking about a nice-looking, well-built blonde with not too many obvious Viking ancestors, Teresa?''

"That sounds like Melina. Do you know her, Dick?''

"Not as well as I thought I did, and, son of a bitch, she was sort of in my neighborhood just before Gaston and me were ambushed! Oh, boy, the guy who said perfidy was a woman must have met a few bleached blondes at a paseo in his time. Of course, it could just get by as coincidence, given round heels in a small town, but—''

"You picked up my grandfather's wife on the street? You dared?'' she cut in.

So he quickly soothed, "Quien sabe? A blonde is a blonde no matter what color hair she might have. The point's not what she might or might not have done to *me*. The point's what she or her pals might be planning to do to you! We're going to have to make our break near a town with a telegrapho. If we hole up good and wire your grandfather to send his own picked men for . . . Nuts, that could be a dumb move, if the lady of the house answers many doors when a message arrives by any means. I'm going to have to study on this some more. It's getting really late. So let's try to get some sleep now.''

He rolled over, closed his eyes, and tried to take his own advice as Teresa fumed silently at his side. She knew full well what she'd warned him not to try. But she'd never felt so insulted in her life.

As any experienced soldier of fortune might have expected, the guerrilla band took a casual approach to reveille and chow call. But it was nice to learn that at least one woman he'd met recently was truthful. Ernesta had not been whistling Dixie when she'd warned Captain Gringo that El Generale was a walking wonder. He indulged his people in a long, warm breakfast, gave them plenty of time to load the pack mules provided for the heavier gear, allowed them to fall in wherever they chose in his column, and then proceeded to march them to death.

Teresa wouldn't have lasted an hour on her feet at that pace. So Captain Gringo sat her on the mule they'd issued him to pack his Maxim and carried the not-quite-as-heavy weapon on his shoulder as he led the mule. Ernesta followed, leading the ammo mule and wearing an expression midway between smugness and resentment. Teresa seemed unaware of her existence, so naturally she couldn't know that the girl everyone thought of as her co-mistress was laughing at her because Captain Gringo appeared to prefer her loving and scowling at her because the lazy, useless blanca got to ride instead of walk. Captain Gringo had gotten Ernesta to donate one of her extra peon skirts and a cotton blouse to Teresa as well, and that hadn't made the peon girl like the highborn Spanish beauty any better. But with luck he hoped to keep peace in his ménage à trois, if that was what one called such a grotesque setup. Jealous or not, Ernesta knew the rules of the guerrilla way of life, and Teresa had nothing to feel jealous about, so what the hell.

Having assigned Captain Gringo his new job, El Generale hadn't bothered much with him since. Nobody had told Gaston anything about his new duties to the cause of Grenada, so he was free to walk along with Captain Gringo and his pretty machine-gun crew, near the middle of the column. With mules in back of them and the ass of another section's pack mule in front of them, they were free to talk, and if El Generale could be called a walker, Gaston was a natural talker.

He kept saying they seemed to be going uphill as the column wound its way through the jungle, not following any trail the soldiers of fortune could make out. Captain Gringo felt less chatty, lugging his heavy weapon. But he finally said, "Okay, okay, I know we're headed west by northwest toward the highlands. I can see the fucking sun as well as you can. So what?"

"So our droll leader told us, last night, we'd be making for the Nicaraguan border. Nicaragua is that way, non?"

"I know where Nicaragua is. I'm trying to keep track of where *I* is! All the major towns in this neck of the woods are either near the sea for obvious reasons or up in the hills for reasons of health. I doubt we'll be passing any towns or even good-sized villages, here in this lowland strip, and we're at least a couple of forced marches from the highlands, even marching this forced. Doesn't that bastard ever take a piss? We've been slogging at least an hour and a half, and he's supposed to halt for piss-call at least once an hour."

Gaston shrugged and suggested, "Perhaps he did not go to West Point. I am more concerned about the direction he's taking us than I am about his manner of getting us there. Has it occurred to you that the next time we are called on to fight, knowing our great leader seems willing to fight anyone, anytime, on sight, we are sure to be fighting Costa Ricans, not Nicaraguans?''

Captain Gringo grimaced and replied, ''That's all I've been stewing about, when I can take my mind off pissing. My back teeth are floating and, yeah, we'll be in a hell of a mess if we wind up fighting the Costa Rican Guard. We're running out of countries where we're not wanted for doing things like that.''

''Eh bien. Since we agree that making la poof-poof at hitherto reasonable Costa Rican troops could lead to a dismal future in this country, how do you suggest we work it when the time comes? The time is coming, we both know, since the idiot in command is either lost or about to go to war with Costa Rica!''

Captain Gringo fished in his shirt for a smoke with his free hand as he said, ''Let's hope Costa Rica doesn't know we're here. They have no reason to patrol uninhabited jungle. So they probably don't. Maybe Verdugo's just looking for higher ground before he tends more to the north. This soggy leaf mold we're on right now is a bitch to march across and, Jesus, if we don't take a trail break poco tiempo, I'm going to piss my pants!''

Gaston lit his claro for him, then suggested, ''Hand me the Maxim, run into the woods, and water a tree.''

Captain Gringo thought, nodded, and did so. As he dashed out of sight Teresa called down to Gaston, ''Oh, where is Dick going? Has he deserted me?''

Gaston frowned back at her and cautioned, ''Please do not shout about desertion in Spanish, ma'amselle. Most of these people understand the language and could misunderstand a simple call of nature, hein? I assure you Dick has no intention of leaving you behind. I know because every time I suggest it, he says we can't.''

''Oh, Gaston, I thought you were my friend!''

The old Frenchman shrugged and said, ''I like almost everyone. On the other hand, I gave up the habit of dying for anyone while I was still very young. That is one of the reasons I have managed to get so old. But since Dick is still young and foolish, let us change the subject, hein? If you are ever to get in shape for serious travel, it will not be avec your adorable derriere aboard a pack animal. You must, as we soldiers say, leg up.''

"What is the matter with my legs?" she asked.

He said, "They are very pretty. Mais alas, not much good for anything but spreading at the moment."

"You brute! I'll have you know I did not allow your friend to touch me last night!"

"And he still insists on saving you? How curious. Eh bien, as I was saying, you must get in the shape of runningness. Why don't you try walking instead of riding for a time?"

"My feet hurt. These peon zapatas are too big for me, and I told Dick I couldn't walk far in them, damn it."

Gaston looked disgusted and said, "Merde alors. I tell you that you had better learn, and soon. Try walking just a little while and then riding some more when your adorable mais très sissy feet give out on you, hein? That way your feet and ass will have the best of both possible worlds, non?"

She thought, then said, "I'll try. Help me down."

Gaston snorted and asked, "Help you down, as I pack a machine gun and lead a mule at the same time? Merde alors!"

"If you were a gentleman, you'd help a lady dismount, Gaston!"

"True, but since I am not a gentleman, what are we arguing about?"

She told him he was just awful and dropped off the pack saddle. She landed wrong and fell to her hands and knees in the black jungle muck. She remained that way, cursing in a most unladylike way until Ernesta, catching up, stopped her own mule to reach down with her free hand and grab Teresa by the hair to lift her to her feet, screaming pretty good. The peon girl smiled innocently at her and said, "I was only trying to help, muchacha. For why do you say my mother was a dirty pig?"

"You call me muchacha? You dare?"

"Hey, what do you wish for to be called, a puta? I see no ring on your finger, princess. So what makes you better than me, eh? You think because our hombre fucks you, too, it makes you better than me? I spit in your lazy cunt, for God knows it does not seem useful for anything else."

Teresa blanched, raised a hand, and hissed, "Why, you little peon snip—"

Ernesta cut in, "Don't try it, slut! I am a peon and proud of it. So I warn you, I can lick a soft city girl like you with one hand. Si, and handle this mule at the same time!"

The argument was ended, no doubt just in time, by Captain Gringo re-joining them at a trot as the guerrillas blocked by Ernesta's mule began to add their own cursing commentary. Captain Gringo told Teresa to get back on his mule, now, and told Ernesta they'd settle it later, rather than in the middle of a forced march. So he had it sorted out by the time El Generale loped back aboard his own mule to demand an explanation.

Since Captain Gringo and his baggage were moving on in good order by the time Verdugo got there, he simply said, "No excuse, sir. It won't happen again."

El Generale looked startled, nodded, and said, "Bueno. It is good to have real soldados serving me for a change. Are you sure you can handle two adelitas, on the trail, I mean?"

"Yes, sir. They won't fight again."

"See that they don't. If you need help in calming the Spanish one, send her to me tonight. She is muy bonito, my mujer has the rag on, and she would be the first to tell you I have a calming effect on women."

Captain Gringo didn't answer. Verdugo laughed and rode back up to the head of his column. When he was out of earshot, Captain Gringo turned to Teresa and said, "You heard what the man said. Are we going to be good little girls?"

She gulped and said, "Send Ernesta to him, then. She started it."

"I don't think he likes her as much. Gaston? You were here. I wasn't. So what's the story?"

"Merde alors, I am only sixty years old, and you want me to explain women? I would call it a simple case of mutual distaste. They both behaved like, well, women."

Captain Gringo grimaced, and since Ernesta was not in easy earshot, he told Teresa, "Okay, let's say the war's over and make sure you don't start another. How did you get all dirty again?"

"It was Gaston's fault. He insisted I walk and I fell down instead."

"I noticed you do that a lot. Okay, just sit still for now. There has to be a better way."

Gaston said, "Let us begin by returning this disgusting Maxim to its youthful owner. If she exerted herself a bit more, she might in time learn to run perhaps a city block without landing on her hands and knees, non?"

Captain Gringo took the machine gun but said, "No," as he braced it on a shoulder, adding, "We don't have time to leg her up. It takes green legs at least a week and a lot of cramps to get in shape. I don't think we have a week. Not unless all three of us, including her, want to wind up outlawed by Costa Rica!"

Gaston said, "True. We'll be très fortunate if El Generale can get us through the day without a firefight. Mais I could not help noticing, when you scampered off just now, that nobody thought to challenge your departure."

Captain Gringo nodded but said, "Where else could anyone have thought I was going? Half of them must have to piss right now too. All three of us, maybe the four of us, would raise more eyebrows if we simply strolled into the woods hand in hand."

"All four? Mon Dieu, are we planning to take Ernesta along as well?"

"Keep it down. I don't see how else we can make it, unless we slit her throat before taking off, do you?"

"Non, and I know better than to suggest you slit the throat

of a pretty girl who's been so good to you. But do you think she'd go for it? She was with El Generale when we met her, as I recall.''

"She's my adelita now. Aside from that, she thinks Verdugo is a jerk-off. I don't think she'll be the main problem. I'm afraid our spoiled little kidnap victim will be the problem.''

They'd switched to English and were speaking softly. So Gaston thought it safe to say, ''Eh bien, neither of us kidnapped her. We have yet to receive a penny from her family, and the cochons who defamed your good name are now dead. So what are we talking about?''

Captain Gringo told him he was a shit heel and went on to say, ''We don't know that all the rats involved in her snatch have been brought to justice. El Jefe sent runners into town to check out our con. So *they* can't be dead. Teresa says she thinks her snatch was set up by her step-grandmother and, oh, I forgot to tell you the cute part. Remember that bleached blonde I brought home from the paseo, the one who could have set us up at the posada?''

"Very fondly. What about her?''

"Guess who Don Alberto's young wife might be.''

Gaston blinked and protested, ''Mais non, a man that old would never survive such an active life. I may have neglected to tell you I had some of Melina after you'd left her in a condition of unsated nymphomania. Besides, she was simply a casual street pickup, not a woman of the hidalgo class. Melina is not that unusual a name in any case.''

"It's not as usual a name as Maria, and how many dames by *any* name could be running around getting laid in Limón on any given night? What's the total population, say ten thousand?''

"That seems a bit high, and I will grant you blondes of even the artificial species are not too common. But the wife of a hidalgo, picking up total strangers in the plaza . . . ?''

"I knew a Roman emperor one time whose wife went in for gang bangs with her slaves. I think her name was Messalina.''

"Ah, oui, good old Messalina. I wonder what ever became

of her after she gave me that dose that time. Eh bien, it is possible we are dealing with a wicked step-grandmother indeed. Mais so what?''

"So if we're talking about the same Melina, good old Teresa could be right about it being an inside job. A sort of stupid one. But Melina didn't strike me as the brightest lady I've ever met. So assuming we can get Teresa out of this frying pan, how do we get her through the fire to her grandfather?''

"Merde alors, getting her to Don Alberto would be soup of the duck next to getting her out of *here*! Why do you always put the cart in front of the horse, Dick?''

"I like to know where I'm going before I hitch up. Melina never kidnapped Teresa personally. She was in cahoots with a smarter crook.''

Gaston shrugged and said, "True, El Jefe. But he is dead. Last night I made sure as I was poking around to see if anyone may have overlooked the contents of his pockets. They did not, the bastards.''

Captain Gringo shook his head and insisted, "El Jefe wasn't the boss. He was just a front. Probably some pimp Melina met before she married the old fool for his dinero.''

"You know this because he told you, Dick?''

"He didn't have to tell me. He was all bluff. He couldn't shoot us without getting approval from someone in town. He had no control over the camp bully who was supposed to be his segundo. He was the face we were supposed to remember if they decided to use us to cut the cards some more with Don Alberto. Like I said, the real brains never left town.''

"Merde alors, you credit the gang with brains? If Melina wanted the only other heir out of the way, she had no reason to go through such a complex charade, Dick.''

"I know that. You know that. Fortunately for Teresa they wanted to make a profit on her murder. Her grandfather's young wife had to offer something besides her ass to get guys to do such heavy work for her. Forget the kidnap bullshit. The problem now is that Melina still has said guys in her stable, if not her ass. Teresa has no idea who they are. We have no idea who they are. So we can't send for help. We have to pop her out of the woodwork under her grandfather's nose, alive and well. Or alive, anyway. I think we can probably trust the thugs he keeps around him for bodyguards and errand boys."

"How do you know?"

"Would he still be alive at this late date if his fortune-hunting wife had control of them?"

"Mais of course. If he were to meet with some tragic accident while his granddaughter was still alive, there would be two heirs left to divide his fortune, non?"

"Ouch. I forgot Teresa has money of her own that would go to her grandfather's estate if she died ahead of him. I wish you hadn't reminded me of that. It means we can't trust anyone on her side but old Don Alberto himself!"

Gaston shrugged and replied, "Assuming we can trust him, you mean."

"Are you nuts? Why would he want to murder his own granddaughter?"

"You just said she has a fortune that would go to him in the event of her death. Loving fathers have been known to rape daughters, even when they were poor. Add it up, Dick. Who would be in a better position to manage this whole mad business than the head of the entire clan?"

Captain Gringo snorted in disgust and said, "Yeah, you're nuts. Have you forgotten all that bullshit with the mixed-up ransom drops? Who ever heard of a guy staging a kidnapping and then paying the ransom himself?"

"Me. I could not help noticing that in the end the so-called ransom wound up back in the old man's hands. Was it the result of a très incredible mix-up on the part of real kidnappers, or was it a ploy to get you and me to sell his story to the police?"

"Come on, Gaston, you and me are outlaws!"

"True, but not in Costa Rica, and I see that until just this minute you have been swallowing the whole story horn hide and tail, non?''

Captain Gringo trudged on a time in silence, trying to see a flaw in Gaston's cynical reasoning. He gave up at last and admitted, ''Okay, we just don't know. Where does that leave us?''

''In a pickled state. May I suggest that we now put the horse before the cart and begin by hauling our adorable asses out of *this* pickle?''

It wasn't going to be easy. Unlike some other self-styled warlords, El Generale took his trade seriously. He ordered one short trail break before noon and another in mid-afternoon. They didn't stop for lunch or the sacred siesta that even regular armies took in Latin America. Taking advantage of the jungle shade, he simply marched their butts off until sunset, and even Captain Gringo was too tired by then to feel like running and skipping. He had to admire Verdugo's professionalism. Maybe the guy had been Regular Army at one time.

As the adelitas prepared supper and/or erected shelter for the night, Captain Gringo found El Generale holding state by his own private fire. Verdugo smiled up at him. A heavyset bozo wearing an officer's cap and a lot of bullets didn't. Captain Gringo had no idea why natural bully boys always seemed to rate the ass-kissing and peon-kicking jobs. But he was not surprised when the segundo of this band growled, ''For why are you reporting to El Generale? Did I give you orders to report to El Generale, Yanqui?''

The older and more pleasant guerrilla leader silenced the bully and asked the same question in a milder way. So Captain Gringo said, ''I have your machine gun under cover near my hut, if that's all right with you, sir.''

Verdugo nodded and said, ''Bueno. Just be ready for to fire

it when, and at whom, I tell you to. Would you care for some coffee, Captain Gringo? Pour the man some coffee, Robles.''

The segundo's name was Robles. So it came as no great surprise when he reached for the pot but growled, ''I did not know this pretty boy was entitled to mess with officers. I thought the machine gun section was led by a mere corporal, no?''

Verdugo shrugged and said, ''I have not made up my mind what to call Captain Gringo yet. He is not even a private until I say so. But I suppose we had better give him some sort of rank. What rank do you suggest, Captain Gringo?''

The tall blond American hunkered down to accept the tin coffee cup with a nod of thanks that was ignored. He took a sip. It was okay. He said, ''That's not for me to say, Generale. You're the one in command here.''

Verdugo liked that. He said, ''Es verdad. I see you understand military courtesy. Let me see . . . it seems odd to call a person called Captain Gringo a corporal. I think I shall make you a captain. That should avoid confusion, eh?''

Captain Gringo didn't argue. But Robles protested, ''That is not just, my Generale! This Yanqui has no seniority in this command! How do we know he knows how to fight at all?''

Verdugo looked at Captain Gringo and asked, ''Do you know how to fight, Captain?''

''Perhaps. Who does my commanding officer want me to fight?''

Verdugo took a sip from his own cup before he said, ''Quien sabe? Do you wish for to fight Captain Gringo, Major Robles?''

The segundo looked startled and gasped, ''*Me*, fight this Yanqui for you, Generale?''

''I did not order you to fight him for me, Major. I simply asked if you wished for to fight him. If you do not, shut up. You still outrank him, so you have nothing to be jealous about. I will not have my officers bickering among themselves like chickens. I have enough trouble with that among the women in this camp, understand?''

Robles gulped and said, "I meant no offense. I was only teasing a new boy in the gang. He knows I was just teasing, eh?"

Verdugo stared thoughtfully at Captain Gringo, that faint smile still in place. Then he asked, "Do you accept the major's apology?"

Captain Gringo nodded and replied, "No apology called for, sir. I got used to worse hazing at West Point long ago. I don't go looking for fights."

Verdugo, still smiling with no real warmth, said, "That is the point I am trying to make here. We live in a world and we follow a trade where trouble comes to a man without his looking for it. We are making good time. The lowland jungle is not as wet as I feared it might be. In another day or so we shall be in the higher ranching country. There will be less cover. Do you know for how to stop cavalry with your machine gun, Captain Gringo?"

The American washed down the green taste in his mouth with more coffee before he said, "You aim low at the horses. May I ask why we're marching into the Costa Rican rangelands, sir?"

"We need horses. They do not grow horses down here in the banana country. I intend to commandeer some horses in the name of Nicaragua. Some Costa Rican rancheros may not understand that I have every right to do this. So they may call in their cavalry, and you will know how to stop them, eh?"

"Within reason, Generale. Modern automatic weapons sure have muzzle loaders whipped, but they're not magic wands, and we only have one Maxim to work with. I can aim it north, south, east, or west. I can't stop cavalry charges coming at us every way at once and, no offense, the Costa Rican Cav is pretty good."

"I heard about you fighting on their side a time or two. The fortunes of war, eh? I am glad you respect their ability. Officers who underestimate people are no good to me. Let me worry about the tactics and I'll let you worry about mowing down such targets as I choose for you. I am not a foolish leader. I do not lead my people into situations I cannot lead them out of. Was there anything else you wished for to speak with me about, Captain Gringo?''

The American downed the last of the cup, placed it by the fire, and stood up to salute and turn away. Verdugo returned his salute, and as he moved off, Captain Gringo heard him mutter warningly, ''No, Robles. Stay here. The grown men in this camp have agreed that it is over. Stubborn children do not get to grow up among real men!''

Captain Gringo was out of earshot as Robles answered in a whiny voice that *did* remind him of a mean little kid. It was a shame that while all bullies were just rotten kids at heart, some of them could really fight. He'd have to study some on Robles. Having the disadvantage of a brain, he knew how complicated camp feuds could get.

He went to Ernesta's hut first, of course. So after he bawled her out for starting up with Teresa on the trail, he naturally had to make her stop crying with a soothing orgasm. But he still had to chew Teresa out. So he put his duds back on and told Ernesta it was the other girl's turn at his bat. She thought he meant it and began to cry some more. He decided it might be good for her. She deserved some punishment, and even a brutal screwing didn't seem to chastise her worth mention.

He found Teresa finishing a tin plate of beans in the doorway of the other hut. She said, ''This food is terrible.''

So he said, ''That's one of the other things we'd better talk about. Inside.''

As they reclined together on the bedroll he repeated his earlier warnings about behaving like a brat or, worse yet, a snob. He said, ''The feeling's mutual, kid. These people have never had anything to feel snooty about. So they're sullen, suspicious, and jealous as hell of people like you.''

''That's what I keep trying to tell you, Dick. How can you expect me to get along with my social inferiors?''

''You're going to have to learn. Fast. I'm not talking about hair-pulling contests because I'm worried about your hair.

We're never going to get you out of here unless nobody's interested in you as you go off to take a squat or something, see?''

"Do you have to be so vulgar?''

"Sorry. I forgot Castilians never shit. These people do, and they resent people who think their shit don't stink. We've got you toned down in that peon outfit, and you're starting to smell a lot poorer. So keep up the good work. Pitch in and for Chrissake help the other women with the camp chores. Stop sitting around like a queen expecting to be served. If these peon girls had wanted to be servants, they'd never have run off with guerrillas, see?''

"I don't know *how* to fetch and carry. Nobody ever taught me. I have not refused for to help, Dick. Nobody has asked me.''

He tossed his hat aside and said, "Nobody asks the adelita of an important soldado to do anything. She's supposed to know. Some don't. Peons raise lazy daughters too. So if you don't volunteer, they'll just think you're pulling my rank on them, and nobody likes that. By the way, I just made captain. Do I get a kiss?''

He'd been kidding. So he was surprised but not upset when Teresa rolled half atop him to kiss him warmly on the mouth. Then she had to spoil it by rolling back, blushing becomingly, to ask, "What does that mean, Dick? I thought you were already a captain, no?''

"Captain Gringo's just a nickname. How I got it is too long a story. With real quasi-rank in this outfit I can pull the same on most of the soldados. I've got a couple left I have to watch my step around, aside from his nibs, of course. But, yeah, things are looking up. By morning everyone will know you're the adelita prima of a no-bull big shot. So it's your chance to work on the other adelitas. I want you to be nice to them, above and beyond the call of duty. There's nothing we can do about you being whiter than most of them, and they'll still be jealous of your looks. But an officer's mujer who acts like one of the girls can't be all bad. I'd get rid of those zapatas too. They're no good to you, and a few days barefoot will do wonders for your soles and maybe make you seem more democratic."

"What a droll suggestion. Our people are not ready for democracy, Dick."

"Don't tell them. They don't know that. What did you think all these revolutions were about, a lack of interesting reading material?"

"My God, you sound like a Marxist, Dick!"

"I'm just a survivor. The guys and gals outside haven't advanced to Marxism yet. They just know they want, ain't got, and don't like it. El Generale doesn't want to redistribute wealth. He wants it all, and the four of us have to be someplace else before the maniac runs into real soldados. Your Costa Rican guys are good. I ought to know. I trained some of them myself."

She wasn't listening to that last part. Propping herself up on one elbow, Teresa frowned down at him and demanded, "Four? How do you, Gaston, and myself add up to four?"

He said, "We're going to have to take Ernesta along. She'll be more useful to us on the trail than here in camp, wailing like a banshee maybe five minutes after we leave."

"I see!" said Teresa, grim-lipped, adding, "I thought she was only trying to cause trouble when she boasted of you making love to her. Oh, Dick, how could you even consider making love to a common peon girl like that?"

"What's to consider? Don't let this get around, but you high-class dames ain't built much different. I told you our only hope was to get on friendly terms with this band, remember?"

"Oh, my God, you *are* an animal! Tell me you have not gone all the way with her, at least!"

"What do you care? Are we engaged or something? I don't talk about my lovers behind their backs. So never mind how far I might or might not have gone with El Generale, if it means getting out of here! By the way, if you . . . Never mind. Dumb idea."

"I'd kill myself before I'd let that unwashed beast touch me!" She sobbed. He was getting tired of her sobbing. He imagined that her suicide threats included him. So he reached for his hat.

She gasped. "Where do you think you are going?"

And he told her, "Back to make friends with the natives, of course. I just wanted to warn you to behave a little . . . make that a lot, better."

He didn't make it out just then. Teresa grabbed his sleeve and snapped, "I won't have it! What has that peon girl got that I don't have, Dick?"

He chuckled and replied, "Probably nothing. I haven't looked. I thought that was the way you wanted it, princess."

"I did, I do, I mean, good heavens, is it simply a choice between letting that mestiza have you or rutting with you like a common woman?"

"Not anymore. Ernesta would get pissed as hell if I turned up your nose at her now. This is getting dumb, Teresa. What harm can it do you if I go on pretending you're both my mistresses as long as you don't have to join in?"

"It's humiliating, that's what it is! I thought I was supposed to be your adelita prima!"

He laughed and slipped off his jacket to re-join her on the bedroll, saying, "Well, hell, if you wanted to get laid, why didn't you say so?"

He kissed her. She kissed back, better this time. But as he cupped a breast in his palm she stiffened and twisted her face from his, protesting, "Wait! I didn't mean it that way. I meant . . . Oh, Dick, I am so confused, I do not know what I mean!"

"You want me to do the thinking for us?"

"You had better. I am not making sense right now, even to me!"

He said, "Okay, let's take it easy, making all the stops along the way, and I'll stop anytime you say so. It's not as if I'm as desperate as some of the guys you may have learned to wrestle with, you know."

"You bastard! Are you saying that the moment I say no, you'll just go fuck that other cunt?"

"Crudely put but accurate. Did anyone ever tell you you have great tits? What's this, an inverted nipple?"

"Only on that side, and not when I am aroused."

"Yeah, you're right. This other one feels normal. Sort of aroused too. What have we got down here?"

"Oh, wait! I think I am about to faint and, no, no, stop that, you wicked thing!"

So he stopped with his fingertips in her pubic hair and let his palm rest against her smooth, bare belly as he soothed, "Okay. I can take a hint."

She sobbed and moved her thighs farther apart as she said, "I wish you would move your hand one damned way or another, damn you!"

He considered just hauling it out from under her skirt. But he knew he'd never forgive himself, even if she did, so he moved it deeper into her lap and kissed her as he parted her love lips with his fingers and began to massage her to full arousal. She was built different from Ernesta down there, bless them both, and from the way she began to move her hips, she seemed to enjoy novelty as well.

He knew she'd start talking dumb the moment he stopped kissing her to get undressed. So he didn't try. It was awkward enough just getting his love tool out and rolling atop her, fully dressed. For a moment he stopped playing with her, and she sobbed into his open mouth. Her muffled words might have been a last protest. But as he entered her she gasped, dug her nails through the linen of his jacket, and began to move in time with him like a real pal.

Thanks to his earlier rutting with Ernesta he was able to hold back longer than most men would have in such nice new surroundings. It was a good thing he could. Like most mixed-up ladies, Teresa took her own good time to climax the first time. Her passion faded on and off as he moved in and out of her. She sighed and said, "I am sorry, I am trying for to respond to you, but...oh, my God, I am! I am! Faster! Faster! I do believe I ammmmmm!''

He didn't. He was no fool. As she lay in limp submission, moaning about how strange she felt, he undressed both of them to do it right. It felt like a whole new ball game, only better, as he crushed her pale naked body under his to repeat what seemed to be a command performance, from the way she was moving and the dumb things she was saying as he brought her to climax a second time. This time he joined her. She felt him ejaculating in her and sighed, ''Now you are mine! I *knew* you had not gone all the way with Ernesta!''

''You did? How come?''

''You just came in *me*, no? Everyone knows a man is through for the night once he comes in a woman, you fool.''

''Oh, right, I forgot you'd been married. That sure felt swell, Teresa.''

She sighed and said, ''I know. I was there.'' Then she closed her eyes and added, ''I am so sleepy, querido. It still feels marvelous. But, well, aren't you going to take it out?''

He'd had no such intention, of course. But a man has to grab for the ring when the merry-go-round gives him the chance. So he rolled off her reluctantly, and sure enough, she rolled over and went right to sleep. He muttered, ''You women are all alike once you've had your own cruel lusts taken care of.'' Then he wiped himself more or less clean with a corner of the sheet and got dressed some more to see if Ernesta still loved him.

She did. He found her trying to sob herself to sleep in her own hut. She brightened as he got undressed to re-join her. She said, ''I was so afraid you would spend the whole night with your other woman, querido.''

He took her in his arms again and told her to banish the thought. But he was going to have to level a little with at least one of them, so as he felt the delightfully different mestiza up he warned her, ''You were right about Teresa being jealous. You see, she feels she saw me first.''

Ernesta grabbed his organ-grinder and gave it a good crank

as she giggled and said, "I don't blame her. You fuck so good. But you told her I must be allowed to share this, no?"

"Uh, not exactly. Like I said, she's sort of unreasonable. So I think we'd better let her think she's my favorite for now."

"But, Dick, how could that be? This is the second time you have come to me for loving, no?"

"I said she was sort of unreasonable. What if we just let her go on thinking whatever she likes?"

The more pragmatic camp follower laughed and said, "As long as you give me plenty of this, I do not care *what* she thinks. It does not feel as if she got her fair share just now, by the way. How many times did you fuck her tonight?"

"Hey, let's not gossip about other people, Ernesta. Did I or did I not save enough for everybody?"

She lay back, spreading her tawny thighs in welcome, to reply, "I do not know. Suppose you show me."

So he did, and it was easy to convince her that she was getting more than her fair share, which was true, in a way. But if Teresa was satisfied with one old-fashioned donging, was that his fault? He still had plenty to give Ernesta, thanks in part to the renewed inspiration their contrasting bodies offered a man. Just thinking about Teresa's pale, slim body as he moved in and out of the short brown Ernesta made him hot. He'd noticed while he'd been laying Teresa that fond memories of perky brown breasts and a love box that gripped differently did a lot for his libido as well. So, if only he could stay alive before he got tired of either of them, he had this particular problem licked. But he told Ernesta not to talk about him licking *her* until all three of them had had a bath.

Captain Gringo wasn't the only one who'd spent an enjoyable night. So the next morning, as they broke fast together in a moment of privacy amid the confusion of the guerrilla camp, Gaston told him, "We have five to consider now, Dick. Tobasca should come in très handy on the trail, hein?"

Captain Gringo blinked and said, "Are we talking about that fat old cook with red hair, for God's sake?"

Gaston grinned sheepishly and said, "Oui. When you are my age, you will understand that there is more to a woman than the way she spreads her legs. They all do that adorably. Mais Tobasca is a fantastic cook as well. More important, she is in charge of the rations. Need one say more?"

Captain Gringo glanced across the clearing where a fat, middle-aged mujer with moon-faced Mayan features and frizzy carrot-red hair was stirring a pot of beans, not looking their way. He repressed a shudder and said, "I love ladies with keys to the larder too. But do you think she's up to much running?"

Gaston nodded and said, "Mais oui. Though I was first attracted to her by the smell of spicy beans, she showed amazing powers of endurance in bed. The poor thing says she has not had a man for some time."

"That I believe. I hope you didn't let her in on any secrets?"

"Mais non. Do I look like a man who was never betrayed by a slip of a kissable lip? The three swiftest means of communication known to modern man are telephone, telegraph, and tell a woman. I recall an Arab girl in Orlan who swore she loved me who—"

"Never mind the bullshit," Captain Gringo cut in. "How do you know that fat redhead's on our side when the time comes?"

"Because I spent a good part of the night inside her, of course. Tobasca is not a deep thinker, and as I just told you, it has been some time since she's had any kind of man and I, in all modesty, am some kind of man. I had her swearing eternal devotion, even before we got down to oral sex."

"Glugh! You went down on that old pig?"

"It was only common courtesy, since she was going down on me, as you Americans put it so crudely. I assure you she is très clean and free of crabs. I looked. Mais forget her personal habits, since she is my true love, not yours. I shall enjoy all her charms, including extra rations, until you are ready to lead on our Macduffs. May one ask when that might be? I mean, a few more nights, perhaps a week, with such a lovely cow might be amusing enough. But between the two of us, I do not wish to make a career of Tobasca."

Captain Gringo couldn't blame him. The old broad was so ugly, she was almost interesting. He said, "We're heading up into horse country. Verdugo wants to steal some horses. If we can steal some horses, we'll have a better chance. It won't matter whether the dames run good or not, and we can pack more rations."

Gaston swallowed some coffee and said, "True. Mais our chances of running into both cavalry and mounted bandits go up as well, non?"

"Can't be helped. Verdugo's leading us that way. So that's the way we have to go. We're too far from Limón for a jungle run now. Teresa would never be able to keep afoot, and there just aren't any handy rivers running the right way."

"Then how do you propose we get her back to her grandfather?"

"Easy. We swipe some horses and ride like hell for the nearest cavalry post. It's hard as hell to murder an heiress in a cavalry post. Once we deliver her to good guys with guns, we can let *them* worry about it. We never signed on to bodyguard her the rest of her life."

"Merde alors, I don't recall signing on at all. What is to stop this très wicked step-slut from doing the child in at some future date, Dick?"

"Nothing, if Teresa can't convince Don Alberto how wicked she is. But like I said, we can't hang around forever. She knows the score. She must have her own friends in high places. It's not our fight. Our fight's over once we finish rescuing her from those kidnappers."

"I thought we'd done that already. Don't hit me. I understand the situation. The next time you screw her, you might ask her if she has any ranchero friends in the high country. Cavalry makes me nervous, even when I know I have not done anything to them.''

Captain Gringo nodded and said, ''Good thinking. At the rate Verdugo's going we might have to do something to the Costa Rican Cavalry before we can make an educated break for it.''

''Merde alors, surely you do not intend to fire on Costa Ricans, Dick?''

''If they're coming at me with sabers drawn? Who are we kidding? If we punk out on Verdugo before the action gets heavy, we'll wind up with his bullets in us. If we don't put up a good fight for him, we'll wind up with Costa Rican bullets in us. What do you think kept me awake half the night, for Pete's sake?''

''You screwed a girl named Pete too? Let us hope the matter does not come up. I will be très damned if I can see a way out either!''

Before they could discuss it further, Robles joined them to snap, ''On your feet, cabrones! El Generale is ready for to move out, and stragglers will be shot!''

As he turned away to give others a hard time, Gaston spat and muttered, ''Speaking of oral sex, one of us will have to take that sucker of cocks out before we leave. Do you desire the pleasure or can any number play, Dick?''

Captain Gringo remained seated and refilled his coffee cup as he growled, ''It's too early in the game. I think I have tacit permission to clean his plow, but it could be a test. Let's just wait till we see how popular he is.''

They switched to idle chatter, in Spanish, as the bustle of an outfit-breaking camp closed in around them. Ernesta came over to tell them the mules were loaded and ready to move out. Captain Gringo asked where Teresa was, and the peon girl replied, ''On one of the mules, of course. She told me she felt too stiff to walk after all the love you gave her last night.'' Ernesta laughed deep in her throat and added, ''The lying pig. I was keeping count as you gave your all to me.''

Captain Gringo told her not to be mean and poured her a cup as he kept an eye on the others. The hospitality was meant not only for his loader. Robles thundered over to demand, "Have you wax in your ears, Yanqui? I told you to get ready to hit the trail!"

Captain Gringo nodded and said, "My section's ready. Some of the others aren't yet. Want some coffee, Major?"

Robles hissed like a snake about to strike and roared, "You dare to defy me, you Anglo motherfucker?"

Captain Gringo got slowly to his feet as others moved in to enjoy the show, attracted by the camp bully's spout. Captain Gringo smiled at Robles coldly and asked, "Would you like to rephrase that last remark, Major? I could almost swear I heard someone refer to my mother, but it couldn't have been you. You look like an intelligent person."

Robles stared into the taller American's gunmetal gray eyes as long as he could, then looked away and said, "As an old soldier, I speak as an old soldier. The remark was not meant to be taken as an invitation to mano a mano."

"I didn't think it was. But for the record, don't ever say that again. I told you I was ready to move out anytime. Meanwhile I'm an old soldier, too, and old soldiers don't stand on one foot flapping their wings while they wait for people they outrank to fall in. The cooks haven't even doused this fire yet. Are you sure you wouldn't like some coffee?"

Before the major could answer one way or the other, they were joined by their self-styled general, who asked, "What the fuck are you two arguing about now, eh?"

Captain Gringo said, "We weren't arguing, Generale. We had nothing worth arguing about. We were just discussing whether we had time for some more coffee. No offense, but people marching under *you* need lots of coffee."

Verdugo smiled and said, "By the balls of Christ, that is true. We should be moving up the aprons of the highland mesas before this day is over. I want you and that Maxim closer to the head of the column from here on. Foothills make me wary. One never knows what may lie over the next rise."

Captain Gringo nodded and asked, "May I make a tactical suggestion, Generale?"

Verdugo's brows frowned, even as his mouth kept smiling. He nodded grudgingly and said, "If you were not an experienced officer, you would be of little use to me. What do you suggest, Captain Gringo?"

The American said, "Like yourself, I've run into a few ambushes. A machine gun has good stopping power, but it's clumsy to run with. If we march into a setup, I'll set up the Maxim on the spot while the rest of you fall back and—"

"You suggest El Generale *retreat*? You *dare*?" Robles cut in.

But Verdugo snapped, "Shut up. Let the man finish."

So Captain Gringo explained, "You move your rifles back and form a line, belly down. If the enemy thinks you're falling back in panic, that's *his* problem. I can cover for you as you spread out and form a good defense line. If I'm still alive when you have your people dug in, I can fall back to join you. Unless the other side outnumbers us at least ten to one, they won't have a chance of rolling over us. Once we've stopped their first boyish enthusiasm I'm sure the general will know what he wants to do from there."

Verdugo thought, nodded, and said, "I like the part about a line of rifles firing from cover. What about you, out front in that exposed position?"

"I'll probably be very nervous, and it wouldn't work if I had only a rifle to work with. The Maxim spits six hundred rounds a minute and I know how to aim it. So I add up to one small target with the fire power of a well-trained infantry squad. On top of that, most troops are rattled by machine-gun fire. It's a new weapon a lot of people aren't familiar with. So they tend to give it credit for more than it can really do. If they flatten when I open up, I ought to be okay. If we're talking about a really big unit of well-disciplined soldados, it was nice knowing you. But at least I should be able to slow them down for the rest of you."

Robles asked in a pouty voice, "What if they have their

own automatic weapons or artillery?" So Captain Gringo said, "War is always a what-if. That's why people win or lose wars, Major. Napoleon could have used a crystal ball at Waterloo. But crystal balls aren't army issue. A soldier has to do the best he can with what he has. If the other side is smarter or has more, tough shit."

El Generale laughed, punched his shoulder, and said, "Spoken like a Nicaraguan. Let us march on to liberate Nicaragua, now, eh?"

They did, and it was a long, rough day. Verdugo insisted on the same killing pace and, worse yet, since the soldiers of fortune were now near the head of the column, they had to be careful about what they said to one another, and of course, they both knew without having to say it that making a break would be even tougher now.

But as the forest floor began to steepen under them, without a break in the forest canopy above, Verdugo did call more trail breaks, and though these were short, the soldiers of fortune got a chance to know the other guerrillas better. Captain Gringo wasn't sure he wanted to. A soldier of fortune operating in Latin America had to get used to fighting former comrades, the shifting alliances of an exitable culture being what they were. But he'd never enjoyed it. He liked most simple Hispanics, warts and all. The educated classes were much like educated people anywhere, good and bad. The peon was a simple soul, good-natured at heart, albeit with a simple view of good and bad, friend or foe. Like the American Indian so many mestizos owed part of their complexions to, *peones* of all complexions tended to accept a stranger as a long-lost relative or a deadly enemy bent on rape and ruin. They found the normal reserve Anglo Saxons considered polite sort of spooky. He'd found the best way to be accepted was to jump in with both feet, taking what was offered in the spirit it was offered and avoiding moral judgments. He knew that coarse humor was to be enjoyed, with a few but important limits to the comments one could make about another. You could call a peon a lazy drunken bum, and he meant no harm when he said that you were fat or farted too much. It was understood that no man who wanted to be your friend ever hinted you had a yellow streak or, God forbid, even mentioned a woman who was at all related to you unless they had been properly introduced.

Hence Captain Gringo didn't expect anyone to mention Teresa or Ernesta, and or course, nobody did. If anyone suspected Gaston had a romance going with the fat Tobasca, they kept any comments to themselves. At least the men did. Since women were not expected to kill one another when insulted, women being the weak and foolish sex, the adelitas were free to gossip a bit. But in a guerrilla band, even the women were a little macho. So nobody teased openly.

That night, as they made camp again, Teresa gained a few good marks on her report card by attempting to help the other girls, to the limits of her abilities. The tougher adelitas seemed touched by her feeble efforts. So though more than one told her gruffly to get out of the way, some smiled at her now and called her by name. An officer's adelita who didn't put on airs was obviously a woman of the people, and she looked pure Spanish too. Muy simpatico, no?

The two soldiers of fortune lingered longer around the leader's campfire that evening. When Robles asked Captain Gringo in a whisper if he was trying to butter up El Generale, the American laughed and said, "Sure. Aren't you?"

Robles didn't think it was funny and moved off to sit alone and nurse his snit. Verdugo was in an expansive mood, now that he was closer to horses, or thought he was. He'd had scouts out ahead all day who hadn't reported horses or anything else to get excited about. But Verdugo said, "We are making good time. All my weaklings dropped out long ago."

Gaston thought it too good a chance to miss. So he said, "Eh bien, one of our party, as you know, has an injured foot. May one ask just what the rules are, should she not be able to continue?"

Verdugo frowned and said, "I have noticed you have one

of the adelitas riding the mule I gave you for to carry the Maxim. That is your problem. I do not have another mule to spare for your section. If the cunt is becoming a bother, shoot her and use the mule as it was intended for to be used.''

''Could she not simply be left behind, perhaps with a few rations and a map?''

''Do not speak childishly, my little French friend. How long could we keep these pobrecitos marching so good if word got around that stragglers were not to be shot after all?''

Captain Gringo nudged Gaston and interjected, ''I don't know what he's talking about, Generale. I'm not about to let anything that good get away from me. She's worth the inconvenience on the trail.''

Verdugo grinned and said, ''She makes up for it at night, eh? I mean, of course, she cooks and sews very well. She is built well for such camp chores. I think I would wish to keep her too. But let us return to important matters. According to my map, we are not too far from a Costa Rican stagecoach station. They are sure to have many horses on hand there, no?''

Captain Gringo had to try. So he said, ''We've ridden the mail stages in the high country, Generale. The coaches are drawn mostly by Spanish mules.''

''Bueno, this far south a good mule has most horses beat. I must mount my people in any case.''

Captain Gringo shook his head and said, ''You have almost a hundred men, and some of your men have more than one adelita. That adds up to at least two hundred mounts, even with some of the lighter girls riding double. No stage station is about to keep two hundred mules in its corral, sir.''

''What do you suggest, then? I must have horses or mules. I agree that it is rare to find two hundred head in one place. So what is wrong with picking them up a few head at a time?''

''The Costa Rican Guard, sir. When people lose even one mount, they yell about it a lot. Would you really want cavalry chasing you with more than half your people still on foot?

Everyone on the other side *will* be mounted. There's simply no way of outrunning cavalry on foot.''

"Perhaps. But infantry can always outmaneuver cavalry in rough country, and I intend to follow the escarpment north to our own country, once I get some mounts."

Captain Gringo objected. "Not after you brush with the Costa Rican Guard, even if we're all riding racehorses, Generale. They have internal lines of communication, including telegrapho. Even if you whip the first military unit we run into, they'll wire ahead, and nothing moves faster than electricity. They'll have someone, a lot of someone, waiting for us this side of the San Juan. Costa Rica is at peace with Nicaragua, sort of. So they'll alert the guys you're fighting to set up on the *far* side of the San Juan. There are only so many places we can cross that border river, and it would be a snap to cover every damned one of them."

"What a joy you are to have around, Captain Gringo. What is to prevent us from fighting our way through to the other side? We are muy macho and we have the machine gun, no?''

Captain Gringo took a deep breath, sighed, and said, "Generale, Robert E. Lee and the Army of Virginia would have a time punching through what's sure to be waiting for you at the San Juan if you let the Costa Rican authorities even guess you're wandering around down here. I thought your plan was to slip back into Nicaragua by surprise. Who's going to be surprised if you stagger across the border shot to shit? That's looking on the bright side. Frankly I doubt you'll get through at all. But if you do, I can promise you heavy casualties and, no offense, this is a sort of small army to begin with, right?''

Across the fire Robles shouted, "Wrong! Once we get back to our own sacred soil, there will be hundreds of recruits waiting for to join us. What you see here, Yanqui, is but the cadre of an army of liberation!''

El Generale lit a smoke and said, "He's young. I still need those mounts. I am still open to suggestion, Captain Gringo.''

"What if you simply followed the higher and drier ridges north, avoiding trouble south of your border?"

"On foot? It would take too long to get there. People are waiting to join us, as the major said, and the dry season is half over. It is most difficult to liberate Nicaragua in the rainy season."

"It's better to be late than never. But, okay, what if we could get some horses in a less dramatic way?"

"I am still listening."

"One of my adelitas, as you know, is Costa Rican. Suppose I ask her if she knows of any isolated horse rancho within easy reach of the escarpment and its tree cover?"

El Generale nodded and said, "Bueno. Ask her. I am not a violent person. But I meán to have mounts for my people. Tell her I need at least two hundred, eh?"

Captain Gringo said he'd do that and got up to join Teresa in the latest shelter. This hut was a little ragged-assed, since they were getting above the palm line. But it was the dry season, so what the hell.

Teresa was already undressed for bed, albeit lying atop the covers as if she'd hoped he might turn in early. The moonlight through the holes in the brush roof above painted interesting patterns on her pale, naked skin. He got in beside her, doffing his hat and jacket but remaining in a seated position as he said, "We have to talk about saving your ass instead of enjoying it right now. So listen tight. I may be able to talk them into letting me take you and at least Gaston on a scouting expedition once we get up into horse country. We want our story to make sense, and you just never know when some wiseass might trip you up. So, for openers, do you know of a serious horse-breeding outfit near the edge of the high mesas?"

She said, "Si, mine. My late husband left me a rancho such as you describe, not far from where the road from Limón to San José drops over the escarpment, Dick."

"Oh boy, that's better than I could have hoped for. But

remember you don't own it. Not until we can get you there. You just know of the place, right?"

"Oh, I see, we are going to trick these outlaws into letting us go. Do not worry. I know how to lie, if I must."

"I don't doubt that. But tell me true, how many head of mules and horses do you have at that rancho, and more important, how many vaqueros and are they tough?"

She said, "I think we have three or four hundred horses and maybe fifty or sixty mules. Most running free and unbroken. My vaqueros are very tough. They have to be. People are always trying to steal horses, you see."

"I just heard that. How many guns and what sort of defenses will we have to work with?"

"I have a dozen good men and, of course, the usual house servants who may not be worth as much in a fight. The compound is surrounded by a stucco wall. Waist-high in places and higher in others. I have a telephone too. Will that help?"

"It will have to. There's no way a dozen guys can hold out long against a hundred, and I don't think El Generale would let me take the Maxim along on a recon patrol, so he'll have that too. But, yeah, there's a chance we could Alamo till help arrives. Verdugo's a cut above the average guerrilla as a tactician. So he won't want to hang around too long. I think we'll go for it. I'll be damned if I can see a better way."

She sat up, clapped her hands, and said, "Oh, if you can get me to my own little casa and telephono, I can call my grandfather and tell him what that wicked Melina did too!"

He started to point out that Melina might have her own version of recent events, as well as a head on the pillow next to the old guy. But that was family business, once he got Teresa safely home, so he said that was a swell idea, and Teresa began to unbutton his shirt. Asking her why would have been a really stupid question, and he'd forgotten what a beautiful body she had, waking up with another woman that morning. So he helped her undress him and rolled into the welcoming saddle with no further ado.

This time Teresa responded as if she'd gotten used to the idea and liked it a lot. So she climaxed almost at once, and when he naturally kept going, moaned, "Oh, querido, is there no end to your lust? I do not wish for you to hurt yourself!"

He assured her that he was in no pain as he pounded her to glory again. This time they climaxed together, and as they went limp in each other's arms, Teresa giggled and said, "I had no idea a woman could come twice in a row. But I love it. I wish *you* could come twice, Dick. The second time is fantastico!"

He started to ask who she thought she was kidding. Then, even as he started moving in her some more, he wondered why he'd want to ask a dumb thing like that. Obviously her late husband had been an uncaring jackrabbit, the poor idiot, or perhaps he, too, had been getting something on the side?

Teresa's voice was warm but firm as she said, "That is enough, my tiger. I would like for to do it again too. But you know it is not good for one's health to make love too often. Even once a night, every night, could injure your heart, and I do not wish for to lose you, eh?"

"In other words, you're sleepy?"

"*Si*, a little. It feels so good to fall asleep right after I have climaxed and after doing it so twice in a row. . . ."

He dismounted gently, not wanting to wake her up, and as she rolled over on her side with a contented sigh, he covered her naked body and got his own dressed. He was still hot. So he could hardly wait to undress with Ernesta in the other hut.

Getting there was more complicated than he'd expected. As he moved across the dark gap a throaty female voice called softly, "My, aren't we busy this evening, Captain Gringo?"

It was Helena, top adelita of the outfit. He'd admired her from afar all day, since Helena was some dish. She was also the private property of El Generale in the flesh. So her flesh was decidedly off-limits!

She didn't seem to have grasped this as she swayed toward him in the moonlight, long black hair unbound to frame her hard but beautiful face. The moonlight did wonders for her exposed breasts as well. She had a right to feel proud of her great knockers, he supposed, but wasn't a lady supposed to keep her kimono a little less open in public?

Helena must not have thought the moonlit corner of the camp was all that public. She reached thoughtfully for the wilted lapel of his jacket as she asked him, "For why do you keep your adelitas in separate huts, hombre? Do you not enjoy orgies? I know *I* certainly enjoy orgies!"

He chose his words carefully as he replied, "I'm sure everyone does. Does my commanding officer know we're having this conversation?"

She laughed lewdly and replied, "Not if we do not tell him. He is asleep at the moment, with his bottle. Sometimes I feel most jealous of that bottle. If you had an adelita like me, would you prefer to drink yourself to sleep, Captain Gringo?"

"You know you're a desirable woman, and you know this conversation could get us both killed."

"Si. If one must die, why not enjoy oneself first? I do not intend to tell him about us, querido. Do you?"

He said, "So far I have nothing to report. Is this a test, Helena?"

"A test? A test of what? I have not seen you with your pants off yet."

He forced a chuckle and said, "Come on, you know what I'm talking about. El Generale sent you to find out whether I would betray him or not. I'm not going to say anything. You can tell him I know my place in his command, right?"

She looked incredulous and asked, "Are you afraid that this is a trick, for to get you in trouble, Dick?"

"Such things have been known to happen. I find it hard to believe that any man would prefer even Four Star Calvados to a woman as lovely as you, no offense."

She preened in the moonlight and said, "None taken. I am glad at least one good-looking man finds me lovely. I know I am a woman of some beauty, and a woman with needs as well. If there was some way I could assure you it was safe, what would you do about it?''

He laughed and said, ''You know damned well what I'd do about it. You know I want you. I'm a man, not a fence post. But I want to go on living, too, and I know if you were mine, I'd kill any man who even winked at you. So I'd better not wink. It's been nice talking to you, Helena.''

''Perhaps we shall talk about it another time, eh, once you get used to your new surroundings?''

He said maybe and got out of there before someone spotted him. A few moments later Ernesta had no idea why he entered her with such a raging erection. But she didn't seem to mind at all.

The next morning went much the same. It felt funny to be tired and bored but worried shitless at the same time. Captain Gringo was used to soldiering. So he was the first one to come unstuck when, as they were crossing an open, gentle slope, a rifle squibbed from the line of trees ahead and a nearby guerrilla spun to the grass like a falling leaf!

Captain Gringo still had the Maxim on his shoulder so Teresa could ride. He let go the mule's lead and punched it in the muzzle to send it back into the trees, as Teresa hung on, screaming blue murder. Others were screaming all around as some ran and some fell while the line of trees up ahead crackled death at them. Captain Gringo didn't worry about what anyone else was doing. He knew what he had to do.

He dropped to his gut in the grass with the Maxim, threw the arming lever, and proceeded to throw lead back as long as the belt would last. As his weapon choked on the end of the first belt, a hand tapped his shoulder and he reached for the second belt, thinking it was Gaston. It was Ernesta. She'd crawled to him in the grass with the ammo. He snapped the second belt in and took time to tell her, "Bueno. Now get the fuck out of here, muchacha!"

"I am your loader, no?" she replied.

He didn't answer. She couldn't have heard him above the roar of his automatic fire. He couldn't see what he was shooting at. He lost his sombrero to a lucky or well-aimed round and rolled over a couple of times in the grass to get away from his own rising gunsmoke. As Ernesta crawled after him he yelled, "No, don't follow me, damn it!" But she did and gasped, "Oh!" when something spanked her behind. She wasn't hit bad, and by the time she caught up with him he was grateful for the ammo she'd brought as well. He snapped in another belt and fired a short burst before he asked her how bad it was. Ernesta patted herself on the ass and said, "Graze. I feel no blood."

He said, "Keep your ass down next time. It's time to move again!" They did. Even Ernesta was surprised when he rolled over her, Maxim and all. So the guys shooting at his smoke from the trees missed him by yards, and better yet, the guy doing most of the shooting over that way now, was firing from one smoke cloud like the asshole he was. Captain Gringo taught him not to do that by firing a full burst into his position, and after that he didn't fire at all.

By this time the others on his side were all under cover and returning the fire pretty good. So Captain Gringo told Ernesta, "I think we'd best start crawling bass-akwards. You go first and keep that sweet ass *down*!"

She did. He did the same. So a few moments later they re-joined El Generale behind a fallen log. Verdugo said, "I wish I had a medal for to give you. That was close, no?"

"That was close, yes. Where's Gaston?"

"He took some of the muchachos around the clearing to see if he could flank them. He did so before I could give the order. If he gets killed, I will shoot him for insubordination. If it works, he gets a medal, if those other guys have any medals. Who do you suppose they are?"

"Don't know. Probably bandits or Indians. Regulars should have challenged us before they opened up like that."

"Es verdad. Your tactic worked well. I confess I almost shit my pants as my people began to run in circles out there. But we only lost four hombres and a mujer, and now we are in good shape, eh?"

The mention of a female casualty spun Captain Gringo's head around fast. But he spotted Teresa not far away, enjoying a digging contest with Helena. It was surprising how ladies could make soft dirt fly with their bare hands.

His other adelita was, of course, still sprawled beside him. He told her to lift her skirts and let him see how badly she'd been hit. She protested, "I have no pantalunes on, Dick!" So he reached up her skirt and, sure enough, she was bare-assed. She giggled as he explored her naked buttocks, then winced when his fingers got to what felt like one hell of a bee sting. He ran his fingers over it, anyway, and said, "You were lucky. Next time I tell you to stay put, don't try to be so brave."

El Generale nodded approvingly and said, "I saw what you did out there, Ernesta. Next time someone calls you a sissy girl, just send him to me."

She blushed becomingly and said she'd only been doing her duty. Verdugo laughed and told Captain Gringo, "She is much woman, and you say you need two?"

Before the American had to answer that, Major Robles crawled over to join them, sobbing, "I am out of ammunition! We have to get out of this exposed position, Generale!"

Verdugo snorted in disgust and told him to for Chrissake go back and ask the women for more bullets. Then Captain Gringo shouted, "Cease fire, damn it!" as something white waved from the line of trees up the slope. Verdugo frowned and demanded, "For why do we not get to shoot on their coward's flag? Did they extend us military courtesy just now?"

"That's not a truce flag, sir. It's Gaston's white planters' hat."

"Oh, we do not wish to shoot *him*. Let us see what he has to report."

After waiting until the shooting stopped everywhere, Gaston stepped out of cover and casually crossed the clearing as Captain Gringo and the others rose to greet him. The Frenchman called out, "Eh bien, they used to be bandits. We put thirty-three men and a very pretty woman on the ground. Some may have gotten away. Not many of the men. They were strung out like beads along the line of trees when we took them on the flank."

By now the guerrillas Gaston had led were coming in as well. One chortled, saying, "It was like rolling up a line of sitting ducks, Generale! This little Frenchman knows his business!"

"Merde alors, I could have told you that," said Gaston modestly.

So in the end the profits and losses came out in Verdugo's favor. He'd lost four fighters and doubtless a good lay. In return he had more ammunition than he'd started with and, of course, the money found on the dead. There were no wounded. There never were in guerrilla fighting. Since the American .30-30 was preferred by almost everyone with a rifle in Latin America, Captain Gringo had plenty of fresh rounds to thread into his exhausted machine-gun belts. Or, rather, to let Ernesta do so. She said she had to do something with her hands while her ass recovered.

El Generale didn't have to be told how unwise it could be to advance or stay put until they knew more about the enemy casualty figures and possible future plans. The pragmatic Verdugo ordered them to pull back and move south a few miles before they dug in in thick jungle cover for now. Knowing they might be there awhile, the guerrillas made better shelters and smaller fires than usual. No fires at all before sunset, of course, since smoke rising above the forest canopy could draw all sorts of pests.

It was after sunset and a relaxed evening meal that Major Robles got silly again. Captain Gringo was seated near

Tobasca's cook fire with Gaston when Robles joined them. The fat redhead was there, of course, but Ernesta was nursing her bruised behind in her new hut, and Teresa had said something about helping her. It was just as well. Robles had been drinking and seemed to be spoiling for more trouble. He gruffly ordered Tobasca to pour him some coffee. When she'd done so, he threw it in the fire and said, "This tastes like shit. Or could it be the coffee is all right and I am just smelling shit? What do you say, Captain Gringo? Whose shit do I smell around here, eh?"

Since Robles was still on his feet, Captain Gringo stood up before he replied, "I don't know. Have you changed your pants since that firefight this afternoon?"

"What do you mean by that, Yanqui?"

"Anything you want it to mean, muchacho."

Others were listening now, and Robles knew it. He snapped, "You call me a little boy? For why do you call me a little boy, Yanqui?"

"Because you're acting like one. You seem to want to call me a Yanqui, which I am. So isn't it fair to call you what you are instead of by your rank?"

Other men were grinning now. Worse yet, Helena and some other adelitas had drifted over to watch the show. So Robles stuck out his chest and said, "You think you are so big because you know how to fire a machine gun. I'll have you know I fired my own gun many times this afternoon too!"

Captain Gringo nodded politely and said, "We all know what you did under fire. It wasn't much, but what the hell, let's give the kid an *A* for effort."

He sniffed and added, "You're right about something smelling funny around here. You really should have changed your pants before supper."

Someone in the crowd laughed. Robles scowled and asked Captain Gringo, "Hey, did anybody ever tell you you got a big mouth?"

"I guess it takes one to know one. I'm ready to back

anything I say, Robles. Can you say the same, or are you just baying at the moon to make us think you're a big bad wolf?''

"I am not afraid of you, Yanqui."

"Bueno. You're wearing a gun and I'm wearing a gun. Your move.''

"You challenge a superior officer to a duel? You dare?"

"Let's not argue about who's superior. Do you want to fight or do you want to get off my back? I don't give a shit either way.''

Robles looked around, wild-eyed, spotted Verdugo approaching now, and called out, "Generale, these soldados de fortuna are trying for to pick a fight with me!''

Gaston said, "I beg your pardon. I did not know the invitation included me. But if you really want me to join in . . .''

Verdugo silenced him, turned to his adelita, and asked, "Helena?''

The hard-boiled handsome woman shrugged and said, "Robles started it.''

Verdugo leaned casually against a tree and said, "That is what I thought. Bueno, Robles. You wish for to fight Captain Gringo, you have my permission. I am getting tired of this bullshit.''

Captain Gringo had, of course, opened his jacket to expose the grips of his .38 but made no other hostile move as he waited. The bully put his own gun hand near the grips of his hip-hung .45 but didn't touch them as he said, "You heard El Generale, Yanqui. This is your last chance to back down gracefully.''

Captain Gringo smiled thinly and said, "I don't back down. Do you?''

Robles didn't answer. Helena made sure she was out of the line of fire and suggested, "Perhaps he needs a little encouragement, Captain Gringo. Why do you not mention his mother?''

Verdugo growled, "Helena, stay out of it." And she

shrugged and replied, "I was only trying to be helpful, querido."

Captain Gringo said, "I can't mention the major's mother, since we've never met. I seldom visit houses of ill repute and, in any case, I hear she's very ugly."

That did it. There was an amused mutter from the crowd, and as one called out, "Hey, Major, are you going to let him talk to you that way?" another sneered and said, "Sure he is. Can't you see he's ready to piss his pants?"

Robles went for his gun. Captain Gringo beat him to the draw and shot him just above the belt buckle. Robles jack-knifed, bounced off a fireside tree, and fell headfirst into the fire. He was still alive, though gutshot, so the results were sort of noisy. As he writhed in the embers with his hair and clothes on fire Verdugo suggested mildly, "I wish someone would finish him off and drag him out of there. He's really starting to stink now!"

Gaston rose, said, "Allow me," and put a merciful bullet in the screaming man's head before dragging him off the coals by his boots. Tobasca poured a pan of soup over him and complained, "Would you please get him away from here, Gaston? Can't you see I am trying to *cook*?"

Verdugo ordered two nonentities to drag the body out in the jungle and bring back whatever he had in his pants as well as his gun rig, of course. So Captain Gringo asked the guerrilla leader if it was over. Verdugo nodded and said, "He was no use to me in any case. You saw how he behaved under fire this afternoon. You will take his place as my segundo. What should we call you? Major Gringo sounds dumb."

In the end it was decided it would cause less confusion if they went on calling him Captain Gringo. Verdugo had enough other things to worry about. They couldn't move on until they knew what they might be moving into. So he sent

out patrols and told everyone else to stay put and behave
themselves for now.

As the camp settled down for the night Captain Gringo
went to see how Ernesta was and how she felt like behaving.
The mestiza had restrung all the machine-gun belts and stored
them away. He didn't think that was why she looked so
unhappy. It wasn't. She said that while her bruised behind
hadn't destroyed her enthusiasm for sex, it had probably
caused her to start cramping almost a week before her normal
period was due and that she hoped he wouldn't beat her up if
she got him a little messy that night.

He kissed her and said, "Some things are better early than
never. You've had a hard enough day, querida. So let's not
worry about how hard I might be right now."

She sniffed and said, "You will spend the night with your
other woman, eh?" So he kissed her some more and replied,
"Not all night. I'll be back once I make sure she's comfortable too."

"Bastard! I know how you intend to comfort her! But go
ahead and screw her silly for the next few nights. I shall
make up for it in my own way, once I am able!"

He laughed, kissed her again, and sat up to leave. Ernesta
sighed and said, "Must you go to her so soon? It has only
been dark a few minutes and, well, I am not bleeding badly
yet."

He knew how uncomfortable it felt to be hard up. So he
took her in his arms and lay her down again. He ran a hand
up inside her skirts. She had the rag on. But he was able to
get a finger on her moist clit, and as he began to rock the man
in the boat for her, Ernesta sighed and said, "Oh, how
thoughtful you are! But are you sure you do not mind?"

He said, "What's the little stink-finger among friends?
Relax and let me fix you up."

"Madre de Dios, you are fixing me indeed now! Are you
sure you do not wish to satisfy yourself as well? We have
plenty of water in my canteen, and I said I do not feel too
messy, yet, inside."

He kissed her to shut her up as he got two fingers in position now to jerk her engorged clit off. She fumbled at his fly to return the favor. That could have led to messier results than going all the way with her nude. So he stopped her. She sighed and said, "Si, you intend for to do it right, with Teresa. For why does the thought of your erection moving in and out of another woman's pussy make my pussy so hot, Dick?"

He told her to think about something closer to home plate, but as she spread her thighs and began to move her hips in time with his massage, she moaned. "Oh, I must be going mad! I can't help wondering what it would be like to watch the two of you fuck as one of you played with me!"

He said he'd ask Teresa how she felt about the notion. That got her so hot, she climaxed and subsided, sobbing and murmuring that she must be losing her mind but that she loved him so and all that bullshit. So he got out of there before she could get him to promise the impossible. He knew three in a boat would solve his current commuting problem in a most inspiring way. But he didn't think Teresa would go for it, so what the hell.

He was on his way to see what Teresa *would* go for when Helena waylaid him again in a clump of gumbo limbo. The queen of the adelitas said, "My hombre is drunk again, if that is what one calls a real hombre. I may have forgotten to tell you the last time, Dick. But I never chose El Generale. He chose me. I have been trying to figure out why ever since."

He gulped and murmured, "Well, you're very attractive, and rank has its privileges. The head man always gets the adelita of his choice, Helena."

"I know, damn it. If you were El Generale, would you choose me, Dick?"

"Sure, you're a very beautiful woman, and, no offense, you look hot as hell."

"I am *hotter* than hell, thanks to being stuck with a man who prefers strong drink to a woman of strong passions!

Nobody is watching this edge of the camp, Dick. Why do we not go into the jungle for to have a little fun, eh?''

"We could run into a jaguar out there. We could run into something worse when we got back. Verdugo may enjoy a nightcap, but he doesn't strike me as a hopeless drunk, and even if he was, you're still playing with matches in a powder magazine, Helena. You know what happens to cheating adelitas if they get caught!''

She moved closer, put her arms around him to rub her voluptuous chest against his, and purred. "Let us make sure we don't get caught, then. What are you afraid of? Surely you do not think I would tell on you?''

He said, "It happens. You could get me killed if someone spots us simply standing here like this. So let's not stand here like this. I'm too young and you're too pretty to die.''

She didn't move away. But at least she stopped thrusting her pubic bone against him as she sighed and said, "You men are all alike. You might not fear El Generale so, if you saw him with his pants off. He is not such a big man where it matters.''

"He's still got a big *gun,* and other guns backing his play. Can I go now?''

"Don't you mean you wish for to come? I feel what you have bulging against my tummy now, and I admire the way it bulges. Let's just do it once, against a tree, eh? You could be in and out of me in only a few moments. You know you want to fuck me.''

He sighed and said, "I cannot tell a lie. But not tonight, Josephine.''

"Who is this Josephine? Have you someone aside from Ernesta and that hidalga?''

"Never mind. I keep forgetting that dry Yanqui humor doesn't play so well down here. No shit, Helena, we've got to stop this foolishness.''

"You call my desire for you foolish? You dare? Do you take me for a toy you can trifle with? I warn you, I am a dangerous woman for to trifle with!''

He'd never doubted that. He patted her back soothingly and said, "I meant I'd be a fool to get involved with you. You know I'd never be able to leave you alone once I'd buzzed in your rosebush. So it's best not even to sniff your roses. Sooner or later we'd have to get caught. Whatever El Generale may be, he's no dope, and sooner or later even a foolish man has to catch a cheating *mujer*, see?"

"I agree our affair would not be without danger, as long as El Generale was alive for to do something about it. But what if something were to *happen* to him, Dick? You are now his segundo. If he were to die, say in battle, you would be the commander of this regiment, and, as you say, the head man gets first choice. Do you think you would choose another adelita prima over me?"

Trying to keep it light, he laughed and said, "Not if I didn't want to get other girls in a lot of trouble. But we're talking what-ifs, not likelies. Verdugo ducked pretty good in that last firefight. So, well, I'll see you around the campus, Doll."

He kissed her in a brotherly way, or started to, then he pried himself loose from her passionate embrace and got the hell out of there, his mouth still tingling and the tingle in his pants downright anxious by the time he made it to Teresa.

She was still dressed. He wondered why. As he rolled her on her back to mount her, clothes and all, she insisted, "No! We can't. I fear my curse of the moon is near, Dick. I began to cramp at suppertime and... You brute, what is so funny about a poor girl's period?"

He tried not to laugh again as he kissed her and said, "I hear college roommates and nuns in convents get to menstruating in unison too. Don't ask me why. Sometimes I think nature has a very nasty sense of humor. If it's true, the whole point of harems could be shot to hell. Remind me to ask the next Turkish *pasha* I meet."

He tried to feel her up, like the good sport he was. Teresa told him to stop, adding, "If you get me hot, I will no doubt let you go all the way and we'll make an awful mess for me to sleep in. Don't you men ever think of anything *else,* damn it?''

He let go of her and sat up to light a claro. The match smelled sort of fishy, as well it should by this time. He reached for a hanging canteen and wet his pocket kerchief. As he cleaned his hand he told Teresa, ''Let's think about how far we are from that rancho of yours right now. I figure we're about forty kilometers north of the Limón to San Jose trail, a bit farther from the railroad, and almost to the top of the escarpment, give or take a few hours of uphill hiking. How are your feet making out?''

She reached down to feel a bare heel absently, as she replied, ''I am able to walk barefoot with less discomfort now. You are turning me into a damned peon. But over forty kilometers, while I am cramping?''

''Yeah, that could be rough, and once we start, there can be no stopping. We'd better sleep on the idea a few more nights.''

''You are going back now, for to sleep with Ernesta, you brute?''

''I'm not sleepy right now. I've got more important things to worry about, like staying alive.''

He didn't tell her about the problem with the hard-boiled Helena. He knew even a dirty look from one of his adelitas could get them all in trouble. But he knew Gaston had to know. So he kissed Teresa, told her not to wait up for him, and crawled back outside.

Knowing Gaston's current address, he circled the main fire and homed in on the smaller smudge fire in front of Gaston and Tobasca's shelter. The fat old redhead was seated near it, tossing another green branch on the coals to discourage insects. She was still fully dressed, or as fully dressed as a lady with such heroic proportions could manage in a low-cut blouse. He asked her if Gaston was inside, and she nodded sullenly to reply, ''Si, he is as far inside as he can get, the brute.''

He frowned down at her thoughtfully, then ducked to crawl

in and see what Gaston could be up to. He blinked and said, "Oops, excuse me!" when he saw that Gaston was up a pretty little adelita, doggie-style.

The wiry, naked Frenchman didn't stop what he was doing as he cheerfully said, "Eh bien, I could use some help right now. This poor child lost her soldado in battle earlier today, and I have been attempting to console her."

"She seems to be taking it very well." Captain Gringo grinned. Then, switching to English, he added, "You think *you've* got troubles. I've got the boss man's private pussy panting for my fair white body, and neither of my girls is in shape for a forced march. Any suggestions?"

"Oui, fuck her. She is going to be très annoyed if you do not, and since she is in the position to spill beans no matter what you do now, you may as well enjoy yourself while you are risking your adorable ass, non?"

"I was afraid you'd say that. Speaking of pissed-off women, how do you expect Tobasca to take this, and would you mind holding still while I'm talking to you, damn it?"

"I can't. I'm almost there. But as you know, I can talk at any time. What is your problem? *You* do not have to talk and move your hips at the same time right now."

Captain Gringo grinned sheepishly and admitted, "I find it a little distracting in my currently frustrated condition. Getting back to frustration, the redhead outside looks mad as hell, and we may need her help in the end. So are your current movements in this dame such a wise move, you horny little basser?"

Gaston closed his eyes, got a firm grip on the younger girl's slim hips, and moaned, "Perhaps not, but, sacré Bleu, it feels so fine! Do not worry about my old and rare redhead, Dick. I feel sure she would rather be my adelita segunda than not get any at all."

"Well, you'd better save some for her, then. Jesus, how many times do you have to come in *that* one, you old goat?"

"As many times as I can, of course. We old goats do not get anything as good as this that often, hein?"

That seemed for sure, although from the doorway Captain Gringo couldn't see the younger girl's face. She'd turned it away from him in embarrassment, judging from the way the rest of her was blushing, but her body was so great, she could no doubt win a beauty contest unless her face was missing a nose at least.

He had nothing further to tell Gaston, and watching them wasn't doing a thing for his own libido but increasing it. So he ducked back outside. He joined Tobasca by the fire, offered her a drag on his cigar, and soothed, "There, there, Gaston is still very fond of you. He just told me, see?"

The fat redhead sobbed. "Then for why is he doing shameful things to that snip, Rosita?"

"Well, boys will be boys. I'm sure you're still his favorite."

The older, less attractive woman covered her face with her hands and blurted, "Do not lie to me for to be gallant, Captain Gringo. I used to be young and pretty. But I know what I look like *now*. I know I am lucky to have had any loving at all from that nasty little man in there. But I can't help feeling jealous, and we both know he will not favor me again until he has a lot more of Rosita, eh?"

That made sense. He still felt sorry for her and, come to think of it, himself. He smiled crookedly and said, "I know the feeling. It can hurt even waiting in line."

She looked up at him, surprised, and asked, "You feel hot and unsatisfied, too, Captain Gringo? How is this possible? I have seen what *you* have for to satisfy your desires with. *Both* are more beautiful than Rosita!"

He knew better than to mention his *third* choice. He shrugged and said, "Anything is possible if you work at it, I guess."

The ugly old broad batted her lashes coyly at him as she asked, "Es verdad? What do you suggest we do about our mutual discomfort in that case, Captain Gringo?"

For some reason she didn't look quite as ugly right now. The firelight on her big brown boobs might have had something to do with it, and, of course, any man might be curious to know if she was a redhead all over. He tried to resist the idea, wondered why on earth he'd want to do that, and suggested, "Why don't we go for a stroll and talk about it?"

She hesitated, then murmured, "You would not tell Gaston?" So he assured her that he didn't kiss and tell, and she sprang up to almost drag him into the woods.

He couldn't tell if she was redheaded all over by the time they got down to business in a pool of blackness on a bed of ferns well away from camp. It was probably just as well. It felt as if he was mounting a lovesick whale in the dark, or it did until he was in her. As he'd hoped, it was true that all cats were gray in the dark where it mattered. Tobasca wedged her fat thighs up to hook a pudgy knee over each of his bare shoulders and bounce him in and out of her surprisingly tight slit with amazing grace.

Thanks to his earlier inspiration from prettier ladies he either couldn't or shouldn't have tonight, he ejaculated in Tobasca almost at once. She felt it, sighed morosely, then seemed to take it as a great compliment when he didn't whip it right out. He didn't have to do any work at all, at first, thanks to her amazing bounciness. It felt nice to just lie atop her, rocked in the cradle of her depth with his chest against what felt like two big pillows while she thrust up at him in what would have been a bone-jarring experience if she'd had any bones at all near the surface of her smooth, fat body. Tobasca rolled her head back and forth in the ferns, moaning that his cock was too big for poor little her as she tried to swallow him balls and all, then came in a vast, shuddering orgasm that threatened to bite him off at the roots.

When they had lain quietly for a time, she sighed and said, "Oh, thank you, Captain Gringo. That most understanding of you. You swear you will not tell Gaston?"

"Of course not." He lied, adding, "I don't want to fight him, and you are the kind of woman men fight over, querida."

"They used to. I was not nicknamed Tobasca because of the color of my hair. In my youth I was considered a very good lay."

He moved teasingly inside her and asked, "You're still pretty good, old girl. Let's see if there's any more where that last come came from."

"Oh, si, si, fuck me all you wish! Pero, won't your other adelitas miss you? I know *I* would miss you if I was used to getting this every night! It is no wonder it takes two for to satisfy you, you marvelous creature!"

He began to pay her back for her earlier efforts in his behalf by moving faster as he growled, "Tonight I think it will take *three*." So she said she felt most happy she was one of them and began to move with him again. She beat him to orgasm, went as limp as a whale could, and as he kept pounding her submissive flesh, crooned, "Oh, you make me feel so little and helpless. You are so big and strong in every way. I admire a man who needs no vice for to satisfy himself. Where did you ever learn to fuck like a toro, toro mio?"

He laughed and muttered something about a friendly cow he'd met one time. She didn't get it. He hadn't wanted her to. She began to buck some more as she came with him this time. Then she sighed and suggested, "I can suck you if you wish. But, forgive me, I am most tender between the legs now."

He declined her gracious offer, saying he was satisfied, too, and helped her get dressed again. She said it might be better if they were not seen moving back into the light together. He agreed they had to be discreet and took his own time getting dressed and back to the hut he shared with Ernesta.

He'd hoped to find the little mestiza asleep. She was wide-awake and naked atop the bedding. As he began to undress again, and this was getting tiresome, Ernesta said, "Guess what? My cramps have stopped. Perhaps I am not off my period after all. Shall we find out?"

He gulped and said, "Let's not be hasty. We don't want to ruin the bedding, and what the hell, it's pretty late."

Ernesta insisted, "It is never *that* late. I bet I know how to get you back in the mood. Ah, you have washed well since visiting Teresa, one hopes?''

He laughed and said, ''I never touched Teresa tonight.'' So Ernesta said, ''Bueno,'' and went down on him before he could stop her. From the way she started sucking he assumed Tobasca had been cleaner than he'd had the right to imagine, and Ernesta was right about one thing. It sure got a guy back in the mood.

The next morning, after breakfast, El Generale sent for the two soldiers of fortune and told them, ''My scouts report an isolated rancho atop the mesa to our west. They have no telephono line and many horses in their corral. A few of us will ride on ahead aboard our mules for to raid them, eh?''

Captain Gringo asked if he could make a suggestion, and when Verdugo nodded, he said, ''We're pretty far south of your border, and unless they have mounts for all your people, we won't be able to move faster than we have been. Wouldn't it make more sense to pick up the ponies peacefully?''

Verdugo frowned and replied, ''What a novel idea! But how do you propose we get them to give us their horses without a fight?''

As Helena came out to join them, looking as if butter wouldn't melt in her mouth, Captain Gringo said, ''Easy. We offer to *buy* some horses from them. If they *raise* horses, they must *sell* horses. Am I talking too fast for you?''

Verdugo scowled and said, ''Si, I am not in the habit of buying what is mine for to take!''

''I've noticed that. Yesterday we took a lot of dinero off those other outlaws we smoked up. What's the sense of having money if you never spend any? There could be other bandits left to fight. Meanwhile, why pick fights with people you don't have to? If we can get them to just sell us some horses, they'll have no reason to fight us or, worse yet, report us to the Costa Rican Cavalry. See?''

Helena did. She said, ''The Yanqui is right. I will ride with you. For to show them we are peaceful travelers as we approach them for to trade in peace. How much can horses cost, and, in any case, we have plenty of money and not enough ammunition for to fight the whole world, eh?''

Verdugo pondered as he inhaled some more coffee. Then he nodded and said, ''I am well-known for unusual tactics. I am glad I thought of such a sneaky trick. Bueno, I shall take a couple of men for to herd the horses, as well as these two soldados de fortuna who look less like bandits than the rest of us. You had better stay here, Helena. I said I would try to get the horses in a friendly manner. I did not say I would come back without them, no matter how those rancheros feel about it.''

He rose and motioned the soldiers of fortune to follow him. Helena followed, too, insisting, ''Idiot. You have to get close enough to talk to them before you can discuss horse trade with them. I shall ride with you. The party will look more innocent with a skirt in its company. If they behave in a foolish manner. I know how to fight as well or better than most of your men in any case.''

Verdugo asked Captain Gringo's opinion. The worried American didn't want Helena pissed at him for yet another reason. So he shrugged and said, ''She looks pretty tough to me.''

In the end she got to ride along, packing a carbine across her dainty thighs as she followed her man, the soldiers of fortune, and two peon soldados. It took the small party the better part of two hours, even mounted, before they topped a wooded rise and saw a modest spread beside a mountain stream in a parklike flat-bottomed valley. Captain Gringo suggested, ''Let me take the lead in this beat-up Anglo suit. That uniform you're sort of wearing might give them the wrong idea, Generale.''

Verdugo shrugged and reined in as Captain Gringo and

Gaston rode slowly down the slope ahead of the others. A dog started barking before they were within rifle range of the stucco buildings and well-stocked corral beyond. A pair of hard-cased hombres came out on the veranda, holding their carbines politely, muzzle down. Captain Gringo hailed them and raised an empty hand. One of them waved him closer. When he was close enough to talk, he explained, "We are looking for horses, señors. Do you have any here for sale?"

The older ranchero nodded gravely and replied, "For *sale,* of a certainty. We do not raise horses for to *fuck.* May one ask where el señor has come from on those skinny mules?"

"We have come far, in peace, and we agree our mounts are not much. What are you asking a head for your fine ponies?"

"Quien sabe? Each horse is a different color. All are good. But some are better. How many mounts are we speaking of?"

"You have two dozen, no, twenty-three I see from here. To save time, what do you say to a flat rate if we take all of them off your hands?"

"The six of you require twenty-three mounts? You should have told your friends we are not cannibals here. We can sell you nineteen. No more. We, too, would rather ride than walk, and the nearest town is far in any case."

El Generale started to grumble. But Helena shut him up as Captain Gringo dismounted to bargain. The rancheros thawed as they saw that he was a serious person, and by the time they'd agreed on a price, they were downright friendly, as they should have been, considering how they were skinning him. But what the hell, it wasn't his money, or even El Generale's money. So they shook on the deal, and Verdugo's men roped the mounts selected together to lead off. As they worked to form the train, some horses objecting, Captain Gringo asked the now friendly rancheros if they had a recent newspaper he could buy from them as well. One said not to be silly and went in to fetch a day-old edition of *La Prenza* for him. He folded it away, shook hands again, and mounted up to follow as the two lead guerrillas moved the long line of linked horses back up the open slope toward the line of trees.

El Generale and his woman followed with Gaston bringing up the rear.

They almost made it. The horses were moving into the trees when, behind him, Captain Gringo heard two shots. He turned in the saddle to see Verdugo hunched over, clinging to his mule's name, as Helena hit the ground farther down the slope. Gaston was riding his way, gun drawn and using it as a quirt to gallop his own mount even faster.

The Frenchman shouted, "Into the trees, tout de suite!"

But Captain Gringo replied, "Into them yourself and secure those horses! I'll get Verdugo!"

He rode back to do so as Gaston shouted a curse and rode on. He could see at a glance that Helena lay dead, even closer to the now silent and sinister housing in the distance. He pegged a revolver shot at the spread to keep it that way and then put his .38 away to grope for El Generale's dropped reins. He yelled, "Hang on! How bad are you hit?" as he got them both moving up the slope again. Verdugo gasped. "Bad. What about my mujer?"

Captain Gringo didn't answer as he loped them for cover, braced for a bullet between the shoulder blades all the way. But nobody fired, even though it seemed like a million miles and a million years to the line of trees. He burst through the scrub into the inviting darkness beyond. He was surprised to see Gaston seated calmly a few yards in. He asked about the others and Gaston replied, "I sent them on ahead with the horses. We have to talk, Dick."

They were speaking English. El Generale might not have been listening too carefully in any case as the American said, "Let's keep moving, then. He's hit bad. Look at all that blood running down his leg. The sons of bitches got Helena too!"

Gaston shook his head and said, "Mais non, I shot her, right after she shot him from behind. I did not wish her to make a habit of it, and you could have been next."

Captain Gringo reined in and muttered, "Okay, if it's safe

to lie him down, we'd better lie him down. I don't think she'd have shot me. I'll explain later.''

Gaston helped him get Verdugo to the forest duff with a saddle pad under his head before he rose to keep an eye on the trees to the west, saying, ''Those rancheros are no doubt as confused as we are, and one never knows about curious kittens, hein? How bad is it and, more important, why did you go back, you idiot?''

Captain Gringo told him to shut up as he examined Verdugo. The carbine round had hit him from behind and come out a lot bigger through his chest wall. Verdugo hiccuped and asked, ''Is it night already? I can't see you hombres. Where are we?''

''Take it easy. You've lost a lot of blood and you're still oozing pretty good. We're okay. Nobody's after us right now, Generale.''

The mortally wounded man hiccuped again and said, ''Hey, I got the hiccups. Somebody get me some water. Helena, are you there, you lazy bitch? Fetch me some water, poco tiempo!''

Captain Gringo had no way to say it gently. So he told Verdugo, ''Helena was hit, too, worse. Don't wiggle around so much. I'm trying to stuff this exit wound, and you're not helping much!''

Verdugo stared blindly up at him and replied, ''They have killed my adelita? By the tits of the Virgin they shall pay for this! Help me up! It is true that she had a nasty disposition and was not as great a lay as she thought she was, but I still mean to make them die in considerable pain!''

Both soldiers of fortune stiffened as they heard hoofbeats coming from the east. But it was only Marcos, one of the men sent on ahead with the horses. He dismounted near them, saying, ''I sent Gordo on ahead and came back for to help you fight. How bad is our commander wounded, Captain Gringo?''

The American mutely showed him the blood-soaked kerchief he'd given up trying to pack the ghastly wound with, and Marcos removed his sombrero and made the sign of the cross.

El Generale opened his eyes again, seeing nothing, and called out, "Attention to orders, men! Until I recover from this scratch, Captain Gringo is in charge! He will show you how to pay the bastards back for their treachery. You will all do as he says or, by the balls of Christ, I will skin you alive as soon as I get over this attack of hiccups!"

It was the last thing he ever said. He hiccupped blood a few times and then went limp. Captain Gringo felt his pulse, closed his eyes, and said, "He's dead. We'll bury him back at the camp. Let's get out of here."

Marcos moved to help but asked, "Are we not going back to wipe that rancho out, Captain Gringo?"

The American said, "Not just yet. El Generale ordered me to take over his mission, not to get anyone else killed."

Gaston waited until they were all mounted and leading the dead Verdugo home across his mule before he mused, sardonically, "Eh bien, I suppose that when one fucks a man's woman, he feels the least he can do is save his life. But now that you've gotten over that foolishness, Dick, is there anything to prevent us from, how you say, making the next streetcar?"

Captain Gringo said, in English, of course, "I never fucked his wife. That's probably what killed him. You heard him turn his command over to me. So now I'm *really* fucked up."

"Mais how? If you are in command, there is nothing to stop us from simply waving a fond farewell now, non?"

"No. We can't leave these people stranded miles south of their own country. We have to get them safely home. Or home, anyway. I don't think my new duties call for another Nicaraguan civil war, do you?"

"Idiot! You owe these guerrillas nothing! They were holding us prisoner until just now!"

Captain Gringo shook his head and said, "They didn't know that. *We* were the ones who were fibbing. They're not bad people, Gaston. Even if they were, I accepted when this poor slab of meat made me his segundo. With him dead it's my duty to take care of the outfit, and somehow I don't think the Costa Rican Cav will understand if they catch a mess of Nicaraguans this far south of their border."

Gaston sighed and said, "Merde alors, and curse West Point ten times! I was afraid you might still remember your misspent youth reading shit of the bull about a soldier's duty!"

"You want to take off, Gaston? There's nothing to stop you now."

Gaston growled, "Oh, shut up, you know *my* old army filled *my* head with the same shit of the bull, you idiot."

Nobody back at the guerrilla camp saw fit to argue about Captain Gringo's rise in the world. One of their own gave witness that El Generale had turned over the command to his chosen segundo, and everyone remembered what the big Yanqui had done to Robles, who *had* ignored the dead leader's instructions.

So El Generale was buried with full honors, if not as deeply as he might have wished, and once things simmered down, Captain Gringo got out the newspaper he'd picked up at the rancho to see if there was anything worth reading.

There was. Captain Gringo read the lead story twice to make sure of his facts, then called Teresa over to his fire. As she dropped to her knees at his side he said, "There's nothing about this outfit so far, thank God. But your grandfather sure has been busy. Someone came back for seconds. They didn't manage their second ransom pickup as well as their first. This time your grandfather's men shot the sorry son of a bitch and turned what was left of him over to the police. His name was Pedro Rojo. Anyone we know?"

Teresa screamed and started to cry. He shook her to make

her stop, and she calmed down enough to gasp, "I can't believe it! Pedro was the capataz of my own rancho! I would have trusted him with my life! It must have been another Pedro, no?"

He showed her the picture on the front page of *La Prenza*. It had to have been taken while he was still alive, judging from the self-satisfied smile on the weak but handsome face. Teresa sobbed as if she'd been stabbed and said, "It is him, my own capataz. I see, now, how my own servants betrayed me. But how do you suppose that wicked Melina turned them against me?"

He shrugged and replied, "Easy, if she's the same Melina I know. Your foreman looks even dumber than me. Anyone he gave orders to would have to obey him. But look on the bright side. It was the staff of your town house in Limón, not your grandfather's, who slipped you that unusually stiff drink. If Don Alberto's servants were in cahoots with the kidnappers, they'd have never caught this bozo when he came back for more ransom."

"I am still sure his young wife was behind it all." She insisted, adding, "Perhaps she was unable to hear everything that was being said in my poor foolish grandfather's house, eh?"

"So far he hasn't been acting all that foolish. It says here that they let Rojo have the ransom, trailed him to guess where, your place, and shot it out with him."

Gaston had been listening across the fire, seated between his oddly matched adelitas. He said, "The plot thickens, Dick. Do you not find it curious that Don Alberto would wish this Pedro person dead before he recovered his grandchild here?"

Captain Gringo shrugged and said, "They gave him the chance to surrender alive, they say. Try it this way. Don Alberto knew the bastards didn't have her anymore."

"How could he know such a thing, my trusting child?"

"Easy. Old Pedro could have told them before they blew him away. Would you want an enraged grandfather to think you were holding his only heir prisoner if you knew damned well that she'd gotten away from your pals? El Jefe sent someone into town to check our own stories out. So they knew where his camp was, and the last time I looked, it had been shot up good, and Teresa, here, wasn't there anymore. The poor jerk-off tried to collect the ransom, anyway. He got caught. He talked. Don Alberto's men had no further use for him. Who likes kidnappers all that much? It says here that he was shot sort of low. You don't get shot in the guts and balls in your average gunfight. But why argue, as long as la policia bought it?''

Gaston thought and said, ''Eh bien. If Don Alberto is in full control of his household, it should be safe to simply walk this young lady home from the dance. If he is not, what then?''

''Good question. We don't know who's in charge of her closer horse spread, either. I think we'd better put that question on the back burner for now. The old man's smart. He knows by now that we're not around, the original kidnappers are not around, so it adds up the way it is. He probably has his own people out looking for us. Our best bet would be to let them catch up and see what they have to say before we turn Teresa over to them.''

Teresa protested, ''How can you be sure of anyone now? If that blond slut managed to seduce my trusted capataz, how can we be sure she has not done so to others?''

Captain Gringo said, ''That's what I just said. Meanwhile, nobody around here knows you're worth kidnapping. So for now you're safe. Safe against kidnapping, I mean. Getting us all up to the border looks a little complicated.''

Teresa looked astounded and said, ''Surely you do not wish for to travel farther north *now*, Dick?''

He said, ''I don't wish to. I have to. They're depending on me to get them home too. They're already overstayed their welcome in your country. Those rancheros we left a dead lady to bury are sure to report what happened to the Costa Rican authorities. They won't be able to tell them the whole story. But I imagine the Costa Rican Cav will want to ask questions, anyway. So we'd better not be here when they arrive."

Teresa asked, "Why can I not stay behind so the troops of my own country can rescue me, then? Surely they will not harm *me*!"

"No, but they'll just as surely try to arrest everyone else, and in case you didn't notice, these guerrillas all have guns, and I don't think even I could get them to lay them down without a fight."

He looked across at Gaston and asked, "Do you think we could leave her with those friendly rancheros for now?"

Gaston shrugged and replied, "It would depend on how friendly they may feel now. If you sold horses to mysterious strangers and then saw them shoot one another up within sight of your veranda, how would you react to a second visit, Dick?"

"Hmm, I guess I'd be forted up and yelling a lot for people to stay the hell away until the troops arrived. Even if we could get her to them unharmed, they might get sort of fresh, assuming she was what she looked like, an abandoned camp follower. I don't think we'd better risk that. You'll have to stay with us for now, Teresa."

"But, Dick, I do not wish for to go to Nicaragua! I have no friends in Nicaragua!"

He smiled crookedly and asked, "Who does, these days? I'm not about to take you across the border. The currently winning side is mad at me, and I'm not too sure how the losing side feels, present company aside, I hope. If I can herd this bunch within running distance of a crossing, they'll be on their own and we can cut back to the first Costa Rican settlement with a telephono, see?"

"Are there any civilized towns along the San Juan, Dick?"

He was afraid she was going to ask a smart question like that. He knew for a fact there weren't. He said, "There ought to be a border patrol post somewhere up- or downstream. We'll worry about it when we have to. Meanwhile, you'd better get some sleep, querida. I intend to move the outfit out at sunrise, and we still don't have enough mounts.''

She nodded and asked if he was coming with her. He was too polite to point out that that was a dumb question. He told her he might join her later and sent her on her way with a friendly pat on the ass.

Gaston said, in English, ''I, ah, have one to spare if you are mad at that one, Dick.''

Captain Gringo chuckled and said, ''I'm not mad at her. I'd better see how my other adelita's making out. Wonder how come she didn't join us around the fire this evening.''

Gaston said, ''The trouble with having more than one is that one of them is always pouting. Come back if the little mestiza is in a grim mood. I have a problem of my own I'd like to discuss with you.''

Captain Gringo got up, grinning, since he suspected he knew what it was and, now that he'd seen her face, Rosita was pretty as well as well built.

He entered the hut he'd been sharing with Ernesta and saw that she lay quietly on her side with her bare spine to him. He put a gentle hand on her bare shoulder, saying, ''What's wrong? Weren't you feeling well enough to eat, querida?''

She didn't answer. He hoped he was wrong as he gripped her cold shoulder harder, to roll her on her back. She didn't roll easy. She was already getting stiff. He gagged in horror as he stared down at her blank, open eyes and gasped, ''For God's sake, no! It was only a graze, you dumb little broad!''

He felt the side of her clammy throat. Nothing. Ernesta was stone-cold dead. He tried to close her eyes. They popped open again, and the soft smile on her face promised to turn into a ghastly grin as rigor mortis set in some more. He covered her with a ragged sheet and staggered outside, calling weakly for Gaston. As the Frenchman joined him he was puking against a tree. Gaston asked why, and he said, ''Ernesta's dead. We both thought the cramps she was feeling at the wrong time of the month were natural, damn it!''

Gaston ducked silently inside as Captain Gringo heaved his

guts dry. Gaston came back out to say, "Oui, it can happen that way, with internal bleeding. The round she caught did not even break the skin. Mais it obviously broke something inside her pelvis. I have seen such things happen before. It can take as long as three days, if the internal bleeding is slow. I am très sorry, Dick. She was a very pretty girl."

"You can say that again, and, Jesus, she wanted me to make love to her, even as she was dying!"

"That might have been an experience one would never forget. But since you did not, you had nothing to do with her death, hein?"

"God damn it, I should have known! I should have *done* something!"

Gaston sighed and said, "There was nothing you could have done. I have seen such internally injured people die in a hospital ward, Dick. I doubt even a doctor could have saved her, and, in any case, we have no doctor or even a first-aid kit here. Do you want me to take care of the burial detail? You do not look well, yourself, at the moment."

Captain Gringo nodded but then said, "Hold it. We'll bury her inside the hut and say no more about it. We've had enough dramatics tonight, and I want to move everyone out early."

"Won't she be missed, Dick?"

"Sure she will, by me, among others. We'll let the word get around as we keep this outfit moving. I mean to move 'em poco tiempo. So let's not get everyone up again right now."

He moved to his packs by the tethered mules and broke out a short-handled entrenching spade. Gaston ducked back inside the hut with him to help. They rolled Ernesta's corpse up in one sheet and moved it out of the way as they dug a grave for it in the center of a hut nobody had any other use for now. Captain Gringo gently lowered the curled-up little corpse into the small, pathetic hole and made sure she was well covered with cotton, as if it mattered, before he shoved some black forest muck in on her, muttering, "I guess we ought to say something. But right now I don't believe in God. Do you?"

"Mais non, my only hope is that nobody could be responsible for this universal mess." But then he made the sign of the cross and muttered a few words of Church Latin, adding in a sheepish tone, "She might not have been as wise as us about this très fatigué universe. She was very young."

Captain Gringo told him to shut up and help cover her corpse. When they'd finished and patted her grave firm, he rolled up the bedroll and gathered the rest of their gear to move outside. Gaston followed and said, "Eh bien, what is done is done. Fallen comrades in arms are best forgotten. Speaking of arms, I told you I had my own problems, remember?"

"For God's sake, Gaston, don't you ever think of anything else?"

"Not unless I am hungry for food as well. I know what just took place may have left you in a Hamlet mood, Dick. Mais I am stuck with two adorable adelitas, and alas, I don't seem to be the man I used to be. I know you wouldn't dream of taking Tobasca off my hands, although she is full of surprises. Mais could I dump Rosita on you, now that there is an opening?"

Captain Gringo swung, but Gaston was never there when you swung at him. As he danced out of range the Frenchman called back, "Eh bien. I see you need time to think it over. Perhaps later, when you no longer wish to kick my shit, my emotional idealist?"

Actually Rosita wasn't half bad, after a day on the trail and a night spent with the sobbing Teresa and her damned old rag. He, of course, assigned her to the position of loader, and if she could move ammo as good as she moved her slim young hips, they had nothing to worry about the next time they saw more serious action.

Both Teresa and Tobasca seemed a little pensive about the new duties of Rosita. Gaston was able to calm Tobasca down soon enough. Teresa called him a brute, a sex maniac, and nobody she intended to go all the way to the Rio San Juan with, so there.

He told her he could not deny the first two charges but that she had to go on to the San Juan with them, anyway. He pointed out that his sex life was none of her business in any case, unless she wanted to take part in it. That was how he found out that Teresa screwed as good while she was having her period than any other time, although the results, as predicted, were sort of messy. Teresa just laughed and said he was welcome to visit his other adelita now. Then she rolled over and as usual fell asleep, secure in the knowledge that he was through for the night.

A lot she knew. They were camped near a stream, and it took him only a few minutes to get squeaky clean. Rosita was so pleased he'd bathed before crawling into her own hut that she insisted on going down on him. She wasn't as tidy, so once she had him up again, he told her he was an old-fashioned boy, and sure enough, she made old-fashioned love just fine. He wondered why Gaston had let her go as she proceeded to screw him silly. After he'd come in her a few times and she suggested that she get on top, he knew.

Rosita was one hot little number indeed, and he doubted if even he could service her and the passionate Tobasca in one night. Thinking about trying helped. Rosita was built nothing like the fat cook, of course, and while her own dark skin made an interesting contrast with the paler, taller Teresa, she wasn't built like poor Ernesta, either. He didn't want to think about Ernesta. Gaston had been right about the fallen. So, as he lay there comparing this lover's charms with others, he found himself comparing Rosita with that naughty Melina back in Limón. That was inspirational. Rosita had black hair at both ends, and it was amazing how differently tits could bounce. But Melina's had bounced nicely indeed, and he felt sort of hurt to think that she'd just been trying to set him up with all that sluttery. He'd felt so sure, at the time, that the bleached blonde really liked him. He couldn't help wondering what the little mestiza he was in right now was thinking as she merrily played stoop tag on his stalk. It was so easy for a dame to fake it.

But if Rosita had some reason for just pretending this was fun, it sure felt good to him. He shoved her off and placed her on her hands and knees to finish doggie-style. As he entered her that way, Rosita blushed all over and coyly said, "Oh, I feel so ashamed this way, querido. You saw me doing it this way with another man, and I was hoping not to remind you of the way we first met!"

He decided it looked a lot hotter from this angle as he started pounding her from behind. Rosita arched her spine and crooned, "Oh, this feels not at all the same. I did not enjoy it as much with your friend, I assure you!"

He said, "Don't talk about my friends behind their backs when I'm giving it to you behind your back. You know you loved it, then and now, thank God."

She giggled and said, "Si, I have always liked for to fuck. Do you think I could be a bad girl, Ricardo?"

"Hell, no, you screw too good to be called bad. Come on, baby, take it hard and let yourself go!"

She did. They came together that way, and he was seriously thinking of some shut-eye now. But he didn't want to be a spoilsport when she got on top again. He just gritted his teeth and silently promised, "I'll get you for this, Gaston!"

By the time he'd finished breakfast the next morning he'd forgiven Gaston. By the time he'd marched the outfit all day, some of them were sure they'd never forgive him.

They'd thought El Generale was a fiend for marching. They now referred fondly to when he was alive as the good old days. Captain Gringo had everything that couldn't walk loaded on the mounts they had now and then walked the hell out of everything else. Gaston was the only one who didn't bitch, even though he liked to bitch. As a professional, Gaston knew that by now the Costa Rican Cav would be trying to cut their trail. When he told this to a malcontent and was asked how they knew that the Cav was after them, Gaston spat and said, "Merde alors, when one on foot knows that the cavalry is after him, it's too late!"

After a few more days of jungle running, Captain Gringo moved his ragged column up to higher, drier, more open savannah country where the risk was greater but the marching much easier. There were few military posts, he hoped, this far north of the main east-west Costa Rican lines of communication or this far south of the border. He put mounted scouts out to spot isolated spreads or settlements before they could spot his mysterious main column. With luck nobody was likely to get excited if a lone horseman appeared on the horizon and then chose to ride somewhere else. When some of the others asked why they didn't try to pick up more horses, he explained that there was simply no way, by fair means or foul, to pick up that many mounts without attracting attention. To mount everyone would call for at least a hundred or more head, and unless they could mount everyone, there was no point in mounting less. Some of the younger guerrillas muttered that he was acting chicken. The older and wiser ones told them to shut up. It was good to be marching under someone who seemed to know what he was doing for a change.

Captain Gringo rewarded their faith in him on the third day on the savannah when, at about noon, a scout rode in to announce armed men, a lot of armed men, coming their way from the north.

Captain Gringo asked if they looked like soldados or banditos and was told, "Banditos, Captain Gringo. Like us, they are dressed in white cotton with crossed ammo belts and too many guns for honest men to carry in this heat."

"Mounted or afoot, Morales?"

"Both, Captain Gringo. Like us, they have horses but not enough. I think, from the way they shouted at me just now, they desire horses greatly."

Captain Gringo had just led his people across an arroyo. He ordered everyone back there to dig in, with the women and other livestock below the rim of the wash. Once he'd formed a fire line across the path they'd been following north, he put Gaston in charge, took the Maxim from its tripod, and picked up an ammo cannister as well. When Rosita picked up two others, he told her, "No, stay here with the others, querida. I'll have enough to worry about, and you dames have delicate asses."

She insisted. He didn't have time to argue, and one never knew how much ammo one might need until one needed it bad. He led her and his extra machine-gun belts up the arroyo and across open ground to a handy clump of chaparral. He put his load down and stared hard at the shimmering horizon to the north. He was about to tell Rosita to scoot when he saw that it was too late. He said, "Lie flat on the ground and don't look up till I tell you to. We have company coming."

He hunkered down in the brush and armed the Maxim as they waited. The oncoming band was advancing in good order, with scouts on foot out to the flanks, God damn them. But he could tell from the way they were following the trail that they didn't know the country as well as he did. The riders arrogantly leading the advance didn't see the arroyo winding across the otherwise flat grassland ahead of them, God bless it. He'd chosen the position with that hope in mind.

Captain Gringo manhandled the heavy Maxim into position with its water jacket braced in the lower fork of whatever kind of semitropical shrub this particular clump was made up of. He cleared the belt and lay it flat-out to his left. Rosita patted him on the ass to warn, "An hombre approaches from your right, Dick!"

He said, "I see him. Let go my ass and keep your head down!" The dismounted scout was in a good flanking position but scouting lousy with his hat brim down to protect his

eyes from the overhead sun. From time to time he looked up.
Most of the time he moved across the grass as if he were
hoping to flush a rabbit. He got quite close to their clump of
chaparral before he looked up again and locked eyes with a
machine-gun muzzle.

He froze in place. Captain Gringo softly called, "You're
doing fine. Walk this way, very casually. You were going to
take a leak in these bushes, anyway, right?"

The scout started to look back at this comrades. Captain
Gringo snapped, "Don't! I can blow you in two before you
can finish yelling mamasita! Drift this way like a good little
scout and we may be able to keep things friendly."

The scout shrugged fatalistically and walked slowly over.
At closer range he turned out to be a not too bright-looking
peon of say forty. He said, "Listen, we are not banditos,
amigo. We are refugees from Nicaragua, see?"

"No shit? Which side were you fighting for with all those
pretty brass bullets?"

"Leon, of course. All the good people fight for Leon. The
damned Grenada forces got the upper hand some way a few
days ago, and we must move through Costa Rican territory
for to get around them and that unfair artillery they got
someplace. We have done nothing bad to you Costa Ricans.
We just need some space for to fight our own revolution,
eh?"

"Come closer. Don't shit me if you want to live. Have you
brushed with any of our Costa Rican military this side of the
border?"

"Pero no. You are the first serious person we have come
across since we crossed the San Juan."

"Then where did those guys over there get those cow
ponies?"

"Oh, the rancheros we took them from were not serious
people. I thought we were discussing military matters."

"We are. Pay careful attention. I now have a pistol as well
as this clumsier weapon covering you. You will slowly drift

around to the back of this clump and lay your head on the grass. Are you listening to this, Rosita?''

"Si, I got my own gun on him now, Dick."

"Bueno. You heard what the lady said, muchacho. Move it.''

The scout started to. Then one of the mounted men in the distance called out to him. Captain Gringo stiffened. The scout wanted to live a while longer. So he waved, pointed at his crotch, and moved on around the clump as if to take a modest piss. The rider who'd hailed him looked away. The scout murmured, ''Buen'dia, señorita,'' and lay down next to Rosita, who took his carbine and tossed it over her shoulder like Henry VIII getting rid of a mutton bone.

Captain Gringo turned his attention back to the column of Leon's own guerrillas. They were within rifle range of the arroyo now. But Gaston was holding his fire for the same reason Captain Gringo was holding his from their flank. They weren't good targets from either angle yet.

Then one of the riders from his higher vantage point spotted movement, or perhaps it was just the way the trail ahead dropped over an otherwise invisible edge. He called out, and the guerrillas fanned out to either side of the trail to form a long, ragged skirmish line, facing the arroyo as a row of widely spaced targets but presenting themselves to Captain Gringo's Maxim muzzle like a row of domino tiles. He knew Gaston still didn't know who the hell they were. He knew he'd never have them lined up so nicely once the shooting began. So he began the shooting, and sure enough, they started going down like domino tiles as he emptied the first belt into them from their left flank.

He snapped, ''Rosita! Make sure that guy stays put and hand me another belt!''

She said, ''Okeedokee,'' which she'd learned from him in bed and found amusing. As he groped behind him she slipped the end of the fresh belt in his questing hand. He injected it and opened up again, this time in shorter bursts, as he had to choose more scattered targets. Gaston and the others had opened fire from the arroyo as well, and the enemy was in bad shape, caught in the *L* of automatic and repeater fire. They were in such bad shape, in fact, that Captain Gringo ceased fire before he'd spent the second belt. There was no point wasting ammo on those already down, and by now the only thing on its feet out there was a wounded horse running in circles under an empty saddle.

He heard Gaston call a cursing cease fire, and as the wiry little Frenchman rose from the arroyo waving his own skirmish line forward, Captain Gringo turned to see how Rosita and his prisoner were making out. Rosita was making out swell. The prisoner beside her was facedown in the grass with a big red stain spread across the back of his shirt. Captain Gringo frowned and asked, "Did you have to do that?"

Rosita replied, "You said for to keep him quiet, no?"

He shrugged. She took his suggestions seriously in bed too. So what the hell. Leaving the Maxim to cool where it was for now, he rose to join Gaston and the others out amid the carnage. As one of their own men finished off a wounded enemy, Gaston shouted, "Merde alors, save at least one for questioning! We still do not know who they might have been, damn your mother's eyes!" Then he spotted Captain Gringo and added, "Who might they have been, Dick?"

Captain Gringo told him. Gaston brightened and said, "Eh bien. If they have run across no Costa Rican forces up to now, that could mean we won't meet any between here and the border, non?"

"It could, but let's not bet the family farm on it. They stole those horses this side of the San Juan. Rosita knifed my prisoner before he could tell me what else they might have done. The purloined livestock alone could have upset people enough to call the law. Let's gather up the loot and git."

"Oui, at the pace we have been marching the border can't be too far now, hein?"

Captain Gringo shook his head and said, "We can't move father north along this highland route. God knows how many pissed-off Costa Ricans must be pissing all along it to the north right now! We'll have to swing east and drop over into the jungle slopes some more.''

Gaston started to argue. But he was an older soldier than Captain Gringo. So he sighed and said, ''Merde alors, just as my socks were dry at last. Our horses will not move as well as we, once we are back among the murmuring palms, you know.''

''Sure I know horses make lousy time in machete country. That's the point. Would you really like to meet up with cavalry in open savannah, for Pete's sake?''

''Mais non. Now that I have seen how these quite ordinary followers of ours shoot, I am afraid to meet Pete!''

The machete work only lasted a few miles down the slope, of course. Once they'd hacked their way through the rampant growth where the trade winds suddenly bounced and dumped a constant sprinkle, they were once more in true rain forest, where the tree canopy high above caught the short, almost daily showers of the so-called dry season. In the more accurately named wet season, the black leaf mold between the wide-spaced buttress-rooted jungle giants would be a slippery slime where it wasn't under running water. But at this time of the year the forest floor was firm enough for easy walking in most places. Captain Gringo swung his column north again before it reached the really flat lowlands closer to the coast. He didn't want to ford any jungle creeks deep enough for a Costa Rican gunboat to move up, either. So after a time everyone's left leg was more tired than the right, since it got to walk on the uphill side. The mules were okay. Mules usually were. But the horses they'd paid such a heavy price for were becoming a pain in the ass as they slipped on the slopes and refused to eat the lush but mysterious leaves their handlers macheted for them.

Worse yet, they left distinct hoofprints with their steel-shod hooves. The unshod mules and mostly barefoot guerrillas left some impression on the moist, black-matted leaf mold. But the spongy surface tended to bounce back and, of course, more leaves kept falling to rot on top. But the prima donna ponies cut through to the brick-red laterite under the thin black surface, and the effect was startling. There was no mistaking a lucky red horseshoe against wet blackboard-black for the paw print of anything one expected to find scampering through a jungle. Gaston suggested abandoning the horses, pointing out that since all of them couldn't ride, the brutes were only really useful to anyone trailing them.

Captain Gringo nodded but said, "Not yet. Any curious cavalry coming upon the scene of that big shoot-out is sure to follow our sign over the edge, and it wouldn't take your average Apache long to spot the trail we cut with our machetes. But it's getting dark, and nobody with the brains of a gnat is about to follow us farther until they can see what they're doing. I didn't police up my brass after the firefight. I wanted any nosy military to guess that we had at least one automatic weapon."

"Ah, oui, even I would hesitate to follow a man with a machine gun up a dark alley, and I am a hero by nature. Mais even as the sun goes down, it promises to rise again someday. Those triple-titted horses are still leaving a line of the bee to our adorable derrieres, and cavalry can ride through these trees as well as we can move the mounts we have less use for, hein?"

"Yeah, but if we turn them loose in this jungle, they'll either die of neglect or, worse yet, follow us like dogs. How can they know we don't have oats we've been holding out on them?"

"In other words, we are damned if we do and damned if we don't?"

"I didn't say that. We can't help leaving a clear trail right now. So we'll leave it until dark and make camp."

"Avec très discreet fires, of course?"

"Of course. Though I doubt anyone could be close enough

behind to matter. We'll fort up and rest all our legs, including the horses'. In the morning we'll move the horses straight up slope from the campsite. We'll turn them loose on the savannah. Where would *you* go if you were a hungry horse?''

Gaston brightened and said, ''I would kiss you if I was that kind of a boy! You are a genius, like me! Anyone trailing us will come upon the cold ashes of an abandoned camp, spy hoofprints sans great effort, and assume we, too, are as disgusted as they with this murky forest and have ridden back up to the savannah to see if there could be a clearness of coast. Trailing hoofprints across drier grass is less easy. If they see any sign at all, it will be headed back to that rancho and . . . wait, why would Nicaraguan guerrillas be headed south, Dick?''

''Shit, how are they supposed to know this outfit came from Nicaragua? Are we about to leave 'em a note pinned to a tree? If they figure out who those guys we shot up were, they'll add up any reports they've had on this bunch and come up with the wrong answer, I hope. With luck they'll assume we're home-grown bandits, and Costa Rican bandits can ride in any direction they want to, right?''

''Oui, so much for that angle. How do we move the rest of us out of camp without leaving other tracks?''

''Very, very carefully. Don't forget that the other side will spot red hoofmarks easily, and let's count on some wishful thinking as well. I remember a time when we were trailing Apache up Arizona way. We had two choices. One led into nasty rimrock where a trooper could break his neck even if there were no Indians around. The other possible trail led across open, easy-riding playas. Guess which trail we followed.''

Gaston chuckled and said, ''Knowing you, I assume you chose the hard way. Knowing most scouts, yours would have preferred the easy one. I get your obtuse point. Mais what if the officer trailing us is smart too?''

''Shit, we don't even know we're being trailed, Gaston.''

''True, but one prepares for grim futures by assuming the worst. The most unpleasing prospect I can think of at the moment involves crack cavalry, well led, sniffing at our untidy trail this moment as we discuss it."

"Look on the bright side. We've still got the machine gun."

Gaston went on bitching anyhow. It was getting mighty boring by the time Captain Gringo checked his pocket watch, saw they had less than an hour of daylight left, and called a halt by a clear jungle spring. He moved everyone to the far side to make them harder to get at and ordered no fires before dark, lest someone spot smoke from the ridges to the west. That gave his workers time to throw together well-thatched huts. Thunder was rumbling off to the east, and they didn't have to be told that the night could be wet indeed for the dry season.

As usual in the tropics, the sun went down with a thud around six, plunging the already gloomy surroundings into total darkness until the adelitas could get some night fires going. Captain Gringo posted guards all around, well out, warning them that if they could see the campfires from where they stood picket, they were too fucking close. Then, having done all he could, he sat on a log near his own fire to clean and oil the Maxim while his adelitas served supper or, rather, while Rosita did most of the work and Teresa bitched. He was getting tired of the spoiled girl's constant remarks about having her own servants to do this back home. So he growled, "Go get the coffee from Tobasca, at least. You told me how devoted your servants were to you. Ask Tobasca not to drug our coffee, and we'll say no more about it."

Teresa said, "I do not wish to drink coffee before turning in. It keeps me awake, Dick."

He snorted, "That'll be the day. Move your ass, sweet stuff. We want coffee even if you don't."

Rosita smiled at him thoughtfully and said, "Si, I, for one, intend to be awake some time."

Teresa made a most un-Castilian remark and went to get the pot as Rosita spooned out the corn and beans. The red peppers Tobasca flavored her simple camp fare with helped a bit. It still would have been uninteresting mush if they hadn't worked up good appetites with their legs all day. Taking advantage of the moment of privacy, Rosita leaned closer to ask Captain Gringo, "Would you like to join me for a midnight bath in that spring, querido? We could go sixty-nine in the shallows, no?"

He laughed and said, "No. That's where Tobasca's getting all her water, and I want everyone to refill their canteens with fresh water in the morning."

"Would it hurt if they assumed there were fish in the spring?"

"Glugh. It's probably too cold, anyway."

"Oh, I don't know. I feel sure I could warm it up for you."

He told her to hold the thought as Teresa returned with their coffee. Naturally she wanted some, after all, now that she'd had to carry it for the peon girl and/or brute.

To keep the party polite Captain Gringo changed the subject to his plans for the less dirty morning ahead of them. He told them what he intended to do about the pretty useless horses. Rosita said he was ever so clever. Teresa said, "Bueno. Let me go along, and when you turn the horses loose, I can ride one home to my rancho, no?"

He said, "No. Weren't you paying any attention earlier today? The country between here and your home spread to the south is crawling with refugee bands from the north, and by now, Costa Rican Cav is out to do something grim about it!"

"Si, but I am no bandita. The cavalry would not abuse me. My grandfather would never allow it."

"What about bandits?"

"I am a good rider. I am sure I could avoid them."

"Alone? Sure you could. You were doing a swell job of escaping when we met you tied to that post in El Jefe's camp."

"Then you and Gaston must ride with me. Haven't you done enough for these Nicaraguans, Dick?"

Rosita frowned and asked, "Hey, pig, you wanna fight?"

Captain Gringo shushed her with a friendly feel and told

Teresa, "Not until I see them back to Nicaragua. It shouldn't take us more than a few more days. Meanwhile, even if you could make it back to your rancho alone, you could wind up dead or worse. Make that dead. There's nothing worse."

"But, Dick, the newspaper said they caught the ringleader of the kidnappers, no?"

"No. They caught a jerk-off trying to pick up the ransom, period. Your foreman might have been the ringleader. He might not have. We mean to deliver you to your grandfather in Limón, not turn you loose among people we're not too sure about. So eat your beans. We have a rough day ahead of us."

Rosita nudged him from the other side and slyly asked what his plans for the night might be. He patted her ass and told her just to start without him if he came home a little late, explaining that he had to make sure the camp was secure before he could even think about sleeping. She laughed and said, "Oh? You planned on sleeping too?" Then she rose to carry their dirty tin dishes back to Tobasca.

Teresa murmured, "Slut. What could you possibly see in her, Dick?"

He shrugged and said, "She came in sort of handy during that firefight. Watch your mouth around her, by the way. She really knows how to use a knife, and I'd feel dumb as hell explaining *that* to your grandfather."

She asked, "For why do you have to say anything to my grandfather once we get back to Limón? Are you expecting a reward, Dick?"

"The thought had crossed my mind. More importantly, I got into this dumb mess in order to clear my name. I told you the kidnappers involved me without my asking to join the party. Lucky for you I did, whether you like it or not."

She looked away to murmur, "Ah, when we get back to Limón, do you have to tell my grandfather *everything* about . . . us, Dick?"

He laughed incredulously and asked, "Is that what's making you so anxious to return on your own, sweet stuff? Do you take me for a total idiot?"

"Well, you have taken advantage of me, and my grandfather is sure to ask if I was raped, you know."

"I don't remember raping anybody. Do you?"

"Not exactly, but we have been very wicked, more than once. You even took advantage of me during my period, you brute!"

"I remember how hard you fought me off. By the way, how are you feeling tonight?"

"I am no longer in that condition, if that is what you have on your evil mind. But if you ever tell my grandfather—"

He cut in to say, "Go to your shelter and think pure thoughts. I'll be along directly."

"You wish for to ravage me again?"

"We'll discuss who's taking advantage of whom later. Get going before Rosita gets back. Come on, doll, move your ass."

She did, telling him how awful he was. So when Rosita returned, she found him working on the machine-gun action again, smoking an innocent cigar. The mestiza sat beside him, hugging her bare knees as she asked where "that Spanish bitch" might be. He shrugged and said, "Turned in early, I guess. She said something about not feeling so hot."

Rosita laughed and said, "Hidalgo girls enjoy long periods. If they worked hard, like us, they would get over them sooner. But speaking of pussy, querido, how long do you intend to fuck with that cold steel?"

He said, "Until I make sure it's not going to turn to soft rust. You've no idea how annoying it can be to have a Maxim jam on you just as the other side charges."

She giggled and said, "I got something that needs jamming too. I may have to take you up on starting by myself, if you do not come to me soon for to make me come. I have been mad with passion since we shot all those men today. Do you know why? I do not know why battle excites a woman between the legs, but it does. Do men get erections, killing other men?"

He grimaced and said, "Some must, from the way they

act. That's one perversion I don't seem to enjoy for some reason. I wish I did. Life would be simpler if I could come that way too. But I'm stuck with having to chase dames when I'm not fighting men."

"I came today, right after I stabbed that prisoner. I mean, I came with my free hand when I got so excited, stabbing him over and over while guns were going off all around me. I begged for you to stop and fuck me in the middle of the battle, but you did not hear me. So I had to just fuck my fingers."

"Yeah, well, I was sort of busy at the time. Can we knock off this conversation, Rosita? I really have other things on my mind right now."

She sighed and said, "Once I start thinking about such things, I cannot stop until I come. Would you be very angry if I abused myself in our bedroll before you joined me, Dick?"

"Hell, be my guest. Nine out of ten people do it, and the tenth one's a liar. Try to save a little for me, okay?"

She said, "Okeedokee!" and scampered off to masturbate. He knew he was going to wind up doing the same thing if he didn't do something about the hard-on he had right now. But jerking off would be dumb as hell, given his current options. So he reassembled the Maxim, covered it with the night tarp, and moved innocently away from the fire, as if to inspect the hell out of something else before he circled around to join Teresa in the nearer hut.

As he crawled in with her and started to undress, Teresa said, "You certainly take some things for granted." Which was pretty dumb, even coming from her, since she lay naked atop the bedding. He stopped unbuttoning to tell her, "Look, if you'd rather I come another time in another place, it can be arranged."

She sighed and said, "Oh, well, as long as you're here, I know you'll just pout until I give in to you. So—"

"Would you like to bet money on that?" He cut in with a mocking laugh. She spread her pale thighs and sighed. "Oh, let us not argue about it, Dick. As long as you have already cut the loaf, what does another slice matter?''

He finished undressing, got in position above her, and inserted his throbbing erection in place, but not all the way in as he said, ''Okay, say pretty please with sugar on it.''

''I beg your pardon? Aren't you going to *do* it, for heaven's sake?''

''Not unless you tell me you want me to. *I* can be a pain in the ass too.''

She giggled despite herself and moved her pelvis up to swallow him alive. But he moved back and insisted, ''I want you to ask for it.''

She said, ''Very well, I confess I do not mind at all.''

''Not good enough. I'm not an animal you're indulging. I'm a human being. I never go where I'm not welcome, see?''

She was breathing harder now. She said, ''You're welcome, you're welcome, why are you teasing us both this way, Dick?''

''Because I don't like teasing. Do you want to fuck or don't you?''

''You know what I want, you mean thing.''

''I want to hear you say it. I want you to ask me to fuck you.''

''I could never say that wicked word.''

''Okay, then I won't fuck you.''

But as he started to withdraw she gasped and pleaded, ''No! Don't stop! Not *now*, for God's sake!''

''What do you want me to do, Teresa?''

She sobbed, closed her eyes, and whispered, ''I wish for you to . . . to fuck me, fuck me, fuck me!''

So he did. He could be a good sport. And once her reserve was broken, Teresa talked so dirty that he was a little shocked, although he tried his best to do what she kept begging him to do. It was simply not possible to shove it up her till it came out her mouth, as she suggested. But he hooked her knees over his elbows and spread her wider to get in deeper than she could remember ever having had any man before. She was begging for it deeper as she climaxed with him. And then he saw he'd created a monster. For that night she didn't turn over and fall asleep as usual. She kept begging for more in a low, throaty growl, enjoying her newfound vulgarity. So he was in her doggie-style, a novel experience for her, she insisted, when Rosita crawled in, swore, and said, "I was afraid this is where I would find you, Dick! Is this what you call inspecting the outposts?"

He kept humping Teresa from behind as he soothed, "Don't be uncouth. You knew I had two adelitas, and the first time I saw you in this position you were doing it with another man."

Rosita blushed and said, "Oh, shit, you have a memory like an elephant. But as long as we are on the subject, do you mind if I join you?"

Teresa, taking it all the way with her spine arched for more, tried to sound ladylike, anyway, as she protested, "You can't be serious! Do you two take me for a woman who indulges in Roman orgies?"

Rosita pointed out that this was Costa Rica as she shucked her skirt and blouse to roll in with them, saying, "Hurry and finish, Dick. I want some, too, very, very much!"

He didn't answer. He was doing his best, it felt grand, but he was thrown off-stride by having to screw in front of a cheering section. Teresa must have shared his distress, though she sure kept her pale rump moving nicely as she moaned, "Rosita, will you please get out of here? Can you not see we are busy?"

Rosita said, "I can't see much at all from here." So she rolled under Teresa to lie faceup beneath her, her head under Captain Gringo's bounding balls as she giggled and said, "Madre de Dios, what a view from here! You sure are getting it good, Teresa. You want me to help?"

Teresa moaned, "Leave me alone, damn it!" as the roguish peon girl reached up to finger her clit and the wet rim

Captain Gringo was sliding in and out of. Rosita tickled his nuts with the other hand as she purred, "Oh, isn't this fun?"

He didn't answer. She was so right. Teresa sobbed, "Stop it, stop it, do you take me for a lesbian, you lesbian?"

Rosita protested innocently, "Hey, what is this lesbian shit? How could you be a lesbian while a man is fucking you so hard, eh?"

"Oh, Jesus, this is terrible! I am being masturbated by a woman while a man . . . faster, Dick! Faster, faster, faster!"

"Play with me, too," Rosita demanded as she furiously massaged the confused Teresa. But Teresa ignored her to shudder in orgasm and fall weakly atop her as Captain Gringo, still trying, followed. So they wound up crushing Rosita as their love mat while she in turn licked both of them as Teresa wept and wailed facedown between her thighs until suddenly she was licking Rosita, too, and a good come was had by all.

As they all went limp and cuddly, Rosita sighed and said, "Will you two roll off and give a girl some air for to breathe? It is my turn with that glorious cock now, no?"

Teresa rolled weakly off, sobbing, "Oh, both of you are just horrid! I shall never be able to face either of you in the light of day after this!"

Rosita said, "Who cares? I don't wish to look at you, anyway, if you have to act so snooty. Can *we* do it now, Dick?"

He said he'd try. Teresa began to bawl when he mounted Rosita. Rosita said, "Oh, hell, move over this way and let me lick you so you won't feel left out."

Teresa said she couldn't, even as she did. It sure looked odd to Captain Gringo as Teresa faced him, kneeling on Rosita's face while he enjoyed the rest of her. He couldn't see anything of Rosita above her rapidly moving chin, and as his passion began to mount again, he had to kiss somebody. So he got stiff-armed above Rosita and kissed Teresa as she leaned forward, bracing herself with a hand on either of

Rosita's breasts so that once again a good come was had by all.

After that, a guy just had to stop for a smoke. So he begged for mercy and rolled out of the way to light his claro. As the match flared he saw that the two girls were now going sixty-nine, Rosita on top this time. It was nice to know that his adelitas had become such good friends. It was kind of exciting to watch too. By the time they'd come again that way, he was reinspired but having trouble choosing, since the pale Castilian girl was just as yummy as the darker, earthier Rosita. Rosita was closer and aimed right. So he mounted her first, and she'd calmed enough to give him a nice old-fashioned lay as Teresa watched, in a detached way, commenting from time to time on his performance until it was her turn to lay him and Rosita's chance to make suggestions. In the end the three of them went to sleep together, each girl resting her head on one of his shoulders as one or the other toyed with the hair on his chest while the other held his privates protectively. It sure beat the commuting he'd been doing up until then. He wondered how long such a good thing could last.

The next morning Captain Gringo and some of his men led the horses up to the higher savannah while Gaston held the fort. They broke out of the line of trees into the open range that hadn't been grazed too recently, judging by the length of the grass between the widespread mimosa and live oak. Once the hungry horses were turned loose on the grass, they commenced to graze. Captain Gringo told his herders not to worry about that. They'd start drifting soon enough after leaving plenty of confusing hoofprints. Meanwhile, they had to get back down the slope without leaving a sign.

That was impossible, in places. But since any trackers would expect to see plenty of human footprints among the hoofprints in any case, they got around the problem by walking backward down the slope where the soil was telltale.

When they got back to camp hours later, Gaston had made the others douse the fires and pack, of course. Better yet, as long as he'd had time to kill, Gaston had had the mules they were keeping led quietly north into the virgin jungle and used brush to scuff over the few marks they'd left near camp.

No barefoot peon was about to leave a footprint in forest duff unless he or she chose to. Captain Gringo and Gaston took off their boots for a while and brought up the rear, brushing away the very few marks they spotted in their wake. They assumed no scouts would circle more than a mile ahead of an obvious change in direction. So once they had their boots back on, Captain Gringo ordered another forced march and the hell with leaving tracks. Whether his ruse worked or not, he wanted to put some distance between his people and anyone chasing them. During a short trail break Teresa, now in a much better mood for some reason, asked how he could be sure that anyone was after them at all. He told her he sincerely hoped nobody was, adding, "If we can get these others to the San Juan without another fight, things are looking up for one and all. Those other bozos driven down into Costa Rica were from the other side in the civil war. So Grenada is on top right now. Or it was a few days ago. It's so hard to tell in Nicaragua. Anyway, once we get to a river crossing, if nobody wants to make anything out of it, we'll send this bunch on alone."

"I hope so. I never wish for to meet Rosita in Limón!"

"I thought you liked her now."

Teresa blushed and said, "I do, too much, according to my faith's teachings. If she ever gets to Limón, she will be in a position for to blackmail me now, no?"

He shook his head and said, "I don't think she'd ever think of that on her own. So don't give her ideas."

"But what if she tells others with more imagination, Dick?"

"Look, she's not at all likely to ever pay a call on a

high-class dame whose address she doesn't know, in another country."

"But what shall I do if she ever does? You should not have made us act so wicked, Dick!"

"I didn't know it was my idea. She's not going to try to blackmail you. If she proves me wrong, you just have to deny it, see? Who'd ever believe that a snotty Spanish dame like you would go sixty-nine with a mestiza?"

She blushed even pinker and stammered, "I—I know *I* would not, if I had not been there. Do we have to do things that way again this evening, Dick?"

"Let's see how we all feel this evening. Right now I'd feel sure I wouldn't want either of you for a month, if I hadn't been there."

By sundown he wasn't so sure. After a hard day on the trail he crawled into the sack just to lie flat while they decided, and they decided one more time couldn't hurt, since they were all going to hell in any case and might as well enjoy the time they had left for such sinful behavior.

The next few nights went much the same, very enjoyable, while the next few days were sheer hell. As they approached the San Juan, the land this far east got even soggier where the timber grew high. He rejected the motion to swing over to the higher country again for two reasons. Even if they'd thrown off pursuit, they were more likely to encounter border patrols in horse country, and, in any case, the high country wasn't all that high as one approached the river running most of the way across Central America from the Nicaraguan lakes to the west.

They spent their last day south of the border cutting through manic vegetation with machetes. So when they did reach the river, they were almost as surprised as the river might have been. One minute the lead machete man was chopping spinach, and the next thing he knew he was clinging to a stalk of gumbo limbo to keep from falling down the red clay bank into the muddy San Juan.

Captain Gringo and Gaston joined the machete crew to

stare soberly across the wide, silent water. The far bank looked much the same. Thanks to the season, the river was low but not low enough to wade in this stretch. When his worried machete boss pointed this out, Captain Gringo said, "What can I tell you, Marcos? The shallow fords will all be guarded, now that the fortunes of war have shifted to the north. Your best bet will be to cross here, where nobody on either side seems to be watching. It's not as if there are no trees to cut down for rafts around here, you know. Look, there's a nice balsa, right behind you."

Marcos nodded but asked, "What are we to do once we get to the other side, if you shall no longer be leading us, Captain Gringo?"

The taller American smiled gently and said, "That's up to you. It's not my fight. Frankly I think both factions are led by homicidal lunatics. If you guys want to go on fighting for the Grenada faction, that's your problem. If you want some fatherly advice, you could just scatter and all go home, once back in your own country. Someone ought to be raising bananas instead of hell, you know."

Marcos looked stubborn and said something about libertad. The others growled the same way. Captain Gringo knew better than to argue. He could see that a civil war between people who called themselves liberals and shot everyone who tried to vote versus a side that called itself conservative and tore down everything in sight was sort of weird, but would anyone ever listen?

He said, "Bueno. There's time to build plenty of rafts before dark. After dark you can ferry across, move into the far jungle a ways, and fort up until you can figure out who's winning and which way you want to march or run."

"What about the mules and the machine gun, Yanqui?"

"Let's not get pouty, Marcos. You get to keep your toys. Just make sure you build big enough rafts. We're keeping a couple of carbines, ammo and supplies, and we have to go home now."

"You are keeping the women, of course?"

"One for sure. She came with us, so she goes with us. I'll ask the others what they want to do. Meanwhile, you'd better start cutting timbers, muchachos."

He moved back to the main column with Gaston in tow and told them that they had time to build cook fires if they kept them small and used dry wood. Then they took Teresa, Rosita, and Tobasca aside to give them the latest poop.

Nobody had to ask Teresa how she felt about going to Nicaragua. Tobasca sighed and said it was her duty to stay with her army. That was what she called it, an army. Rosita hesitated. She asked Teresa about the job situation in Limón. When the Spanish girl said she could no doubt find employment as a house chica there, Rosita swore and said, "Shit, I am a soldada, not a cleaner of other women's houses!" So Captain Gringo said he understood and forgave her for putting duty above passion. It felt great to have something turn out right for a change.

They all went back to enjoy a last meal together. Captain Gringo broke out some ammo for the carbines they'd be taking with them and gave the old Maxim a last once-over before surrendering it back to La Caza. It was getting dark when Marcos joined them to say, "The rafts are ready. Ah, the muchachos have elected me as leader now."

Captain Gringo nodded and said, "Bueno. They made a wise choice. I'm sure you'll get them all safely home or wherever. We'll just camp here for the night and head back when it's light again."

"It is a long way. What if you run into those Costa Ricans we have worked so hard for to avoid?"

"If we can't avoid them, we'll probably be able to bullshit them. La señorita, here, is Costa Rican, and neither of us are wanted by them for anything they know about."

"Perhaps, but what if they make you *talk*?"

"What's to talk about? By morning you guys will be out of their reach in any case. By the way, do you know how to fire that Maxim?"

"Rosita says she does, after watching you. For why do you ask?"

"If you're afraid someone might trail you across the border, you might want to set it up on the far bank to cover your rear until you know you're safe. Do you want me to show you how it works? The head spacing can be a little tricky."

Marcos shrugged and said, "The woman knows all about such things. In a pinch I know how to pull any trigger. We have to start moving out now. I am sorry we must part, after all the times we shared."

Captain Gringo shook hands with the new leader and told him to go with God. As Marcos turned away Gaston observed, "Eh bien, that one has something sneaky going on behind the eyeballs, Dick!"

"I noticed. Let's hope he just felt awkward. I know I did. He'd be dumb to turn on us now."

"Merde alors, do any of them look smart? Consider where they wish to go, and why, when it's so much safer and almost as profitable shining shoes!"

Captain Gringo rose, stretched, and helped Teresa to her feet, saying, "Okay, gang. Let's move it back along the trail a ways."

Gaston didn't argue. Teresa looked blank and said, "You just told them we would stay here for the night, no?"

The American said, "I don't always mean what I say. It's a good thing I don't. We'd never get your grandfather's approval. What we're really going to do goes like so: We fort up and sit tight until the others leave. Then we get to work with our own little machetes and build our own raft, farther downstream. Then we do some moonlight drifting on our own."

"But, Dick, you said we would follow this trail back?"

"Jesus, haven't you been bitching about all this walking, kitten? Why walk when you can ride? There are fishing villages on both sides of the river mouth. We'll stick with the ones on this side. Then we'll hire a lugger to run us down the coast to Limón the easy way."

Teresa clapped her hands like a little girl and said, "Oh, it is all so simple once you point it out! But for why did you have to fib to our comrades about your plans just now?"

"Make that 'former comrades,' and let's hope I was just using a rubber in a hole I wasn't sure of. How far do you think we ought to go, Gaston?"

The Frenchman grunted. "This pack is très fatigué. A quarter kilometer should do it. Nobody is about to stroll that far unless he means something more serious than taking the pee pee, non?"

"Yeah, we don't want to get too far from the river, and I still hope we're being overcautious."

He led the way until he spotted a nice fallen log off to the left of the trail and said, "Here we go. The growth's too thick on the far side for anyone to sneak up behind us."

The three of them piled their gear on the far side of the mossy log and joined it there. He told Teresa to keep her head down as he and Gaston casually braced their carbines to cover the trail and the wall of solid greenery beyond. The green was starting to turn black, and Teresa had just told them that they were crazy and that a bug was crawling up her leg when Captain Gringo hissed, "Silencio! We have visitors."

It was Marcos, a couple of other guys, and yeah, Rosita, and the Maxim. Captain Gringo wanted to get it settled, so he called out in a pleasant enough tone, "Going somewhere, amigos y amigas?"

Marcos hissed a command, and his followers, including the girl, fanned out to take cover. Captain Gringo sighed and said, "How soon they forget. Hey, Rosita?"

"I am sorry, Dick. I love you, as you know, but Marcos is right. You know too much."

"I was afraid you might come up with that dumb idea. But, no shit, Rosita, don't fire that machine gun at us. I mean it."

She must not have thought he was in charge anymore. Marcos told her to see what a full burst would do to their log.

So naturally Rosita took aim from behind a buttress root, tried to fire a full burst, and naturally wound up dead.

As the rear action of the Maxim blew up in Rosita's face, Marcos staggered out into open view, blood streaming through his fingers as he tried to hold an eyeball in. Gaston shot him. Captain Gringo fired at the sound of crashing on the far side of the trail and was rewarded for his efforts by the sound of an anguished scream and no more sounds of running. He grimaced and said, "At least one got away. Let's hope he delivers the right message."

Teresa raised her eyes above the log. She saw the distant hand of Rosita, sprawled like a stomped pink spider on the now bloody trail.

Teresa gasped. "How did you do that, Dick?"

So he said, "I told her not to fire. But you may have noticed how willful she could be. I changed the head spacing on the Maxim before I turned it over to more careless children. It was no use to us now but is still a wicked toy to leave around the house. I was hoping they wouldn't fire it until they got back to their own army and someone who knew better. But they didn't. So that's that."

"Oh, my God, she is still bleeding over there! What is this head thing you did to her poor head? I fail to understand, Dick."

"So did she. That's why her head's still draining. There's a plate in the automatic bolt action. It adjusts to take longer or shorter rounds. If it's screwed too tight, guess what happens?"

"I do not have to guess. Is there no end to your trickery, Dick?"

"I hope not. Guys in my line of work wind up dead when they run out of tricks, querida."

There were no further attempts on their lives by their erstwhile friends. Most of the others had thought it was a

dumb idea in the first place, elected a new, smarter leader,
and did what they'd been told to do by Captain Gringo. Once
it was dark enough for scouting, Captain Gringo left Teresa
with Gaston to check and, sure enough, found that the
guerrillas had crossed the San Juan to a fate unknown.

After that it was what Gaston called soup of the duck to cut
a few soft balsa logs, lash them together, and float down the
river themselves. The current carried them to the broad mouth
by dawn, and they poled ashore at a friendly fishing village
where things got even friendlier when they flashed some
dinero. A couple of fishermen with a seagoing lugger and
nothing better to do agreed to take them down to Limón.
There was no telephone or telegraph from here to there, but
Teresa relaxed once she saw that they were making good time
across the constant trade winds and that the cabin she was
given to share with Captain Gringo in the bows had a lock on
the door.

He assured her he understood that this honeymoon cruise,
if that was the proper name for it, was to be the last time they
could be so wicked. But by the time they were putting into
Limón, Teresa had her duds and her snooty expression back
in place. She warned him that her grandfather would kill
them both if he ever found out they'd been more than
platonic. He told her to stop harping on the subject. He knew
the rules and he just wanted to get it over with.

At Captain Gringo's suggestion the lugger put in at the less
fashionable end of the quay. He paid them off and hailed a
passing hack to take Teresa to Don Alberto's town house. It
was getting dark again when they arrived. He'd planned it
that way.

Gaston suggested sneaking around to the back. He told him
not to be silly and led Teresa to the front door, explaining,
"Even wicked step-grandmothers have to be careful about
gunning people down in the street."

The door opened. The guy inside was one of the goons he
and Gaston had tangled with earlier. That was a break. They
knew whose side he was on. He looked astounded to see

Teresa and hauled all three of them in, explaining, "You just missed El Patron! He has gone up to the highlands for to look for la señora!"

Captain Gringo asked, "Can you reach him by telephone?" and the tough said, "Not this momento. We can leave a message for him at the railroad station up there, of course."

"Bueno. Do that. We'll stay with la señora until we know she's been safely delivered. Speaking of señoras, where's this one's loving step-grandmother at the moment?"

"La Señora Montalban is right upstairs, of course. I shall tell her you are here before I go for to telephone El Patron!"

Teresa whimpered, "Pero no! I do not wish to see her until my grandfather is here!" But Captain Gringo shook his head and said, "That sounds rude. We may as well have it out with all concerned, Teresa. Let's see what she has to say."

The hireling led them into a drawing room and told them he'd get the lady of the house. As the two soldiers of fortune took seats and lit up, Teresa paced nervously and insisted, "I am frightened! You have no idea how treacherous she can be, Dick."

He said, "We're both armed and treacherous too. Sit down and take a load off it. If it's the same Melina I know, *she's* going to be sort of nervous too."

It wasn't. The door opened, and a poised young blonde came in to greet Teresa with a big hug, saying, "I am so happy you have been rescued, my poor darling! Was it too awful for you, dear Teresa?"

Captain Gringo stared in wonder at the beautiful young wife of old Don Alberto. Whatever this blonde was, she wasn't *cheap*. It took lots of dinero to hang jewelry like that on any dame. Her beige silk gown was cut low, and the diamonds winking out between her proud cleavage were worth a fortune. The boobs weren't bad, either.

She let Teresa go and turned to them as they both rose, saying, "You must be the brave caballeros my husband sent for to rescue the child. He told me about you. You must stay until we can call him back from another wild-goose chase, eh? I am sure he wishes for to reward you properly!''

Teresa backed against the stucco wall and hissed, ''They most certainly won't leave me here at *your* mercy, you bitch!''

Melina Montalban looked startled and asked, ''What on earth are you talking about, you poor thing? Since you bring the matter up in front of strangers, let us agree that we have never been too fond of one another. But I have done nothing calling for such an insulting term, even in private!''

Teresa shook her head and sneered. ''It's no use pretending now. We know all about your plan to have me kidnapped, you bitch or, if that does not suit you, puta!''

Melina gasped and would have slapped Teresa had not Captain Gringo moved between them, soothing, ''Now girls, let's be nice.''

The blonde insisted, ''She just accused me of a crime! I won't have it! We have been worried sick about her, and now she says *I* had something to do with . . . whatever happened. I confess I am most confused right now. The last thing I expected her to say was that I was a kidnapper!''

He said, ''Yeah, I'd better explain. Gaston, watch the door. We don't want anyone listening while we rehash a little family business.''

As Gaston did so, the blonde asked, ''Do you know what this is all about, Captain Gringo?''

So he said, ''I didn't, for sure, until you walked in just now. I was supposed to think Don Alberto's wife was a cheap tramp who picked up guys at the paseo. I was supposed to think a lot of things, I guess.''

Teresa sobbed. ''Dick, you have to keep her from hurting me. You must not listen to a thing she says!''

He said, ''Sit down and shut up. She hasn't said anything. That's because she doesn't *know* anything. Game's over, toots. But if you're a very good little girl, we may still be able to keep this in the family. Your partners in crime are all dead, and you didn't do all that much. So maybe your wicked step-grandmother will forgive you.''

Teresa buried her face in her hands and began to sob for effect. Captain Gringo turned back to the more sensible woman and said, "I guess I'd better start at the beginning.''

She said, "I wish you would.''

So he said, "Once upon a time there was a little girl named Teresa. Her mama was dead, her poppa was dead, even her husband was dead. But she had a grandfather. A very rich one. She was his only heir. Or she was until he married a wicked step-grandmother.''

"Do I look wicked, Captain Gringo?''

"Call me Dick. You'd have looked wicked wearing wings and a halo. Because when Don Alberto goes, all he has goes to you. She tried to con us with some jazz about you being the heir to *her* fortune. But I couldn't help wondering why even a wicked step-grandmother would risk a serious crime and a very annoyed husband to get her greedy mitts on a lousy little horse ranch when she was *already* stinking rich.''

"I could have told you that. I have money in my own right.''

"Never mind. Even if you'd been a cheap tramp, you'd still be the heir to the Montalban fortune and Teresa wouldn't. So she and her foreman, no doubt a good friend, cooked up a wild plan to make you look bad and pick up a little spending money while they were about it. I don't think Teresa was interested in the ransom, but she had to offer old Pedro something better than . . . Never mind.''

"I know about 'never mind.' I have been married before. But in what way was a staged kidnapping supposed to reflect on *me*, Dick?''

"You were being framed. First they hired a blonde who looked a little bit like you to use your name when she picked up guys in a trampy way, free. Her pimp was probably the one posing as El Jefe. Never mind how I know all this. Suffice it to say that I was now in a position to tell Don Alberto that I might have tripped over his young cheating wife once I put two and two together to get, say, eight and a half.''

"Was this other Melina any good?" asked the real Melina with an amused but frosty smile.

He smiled back, sheepishly, and replied, "It wouldn't have worked if I really met you. I just did and it didn't. After establishing that you were a cheap bimbo with no brains, they dragged us into the caper by using *my* name on a dumb ransom note. I did just what they expected. Thank God your husband was as cool as they expected him to be, señora. Then, once they had Gaston and me interested in rescuing his granddaughter, they kidnapped us so we could do so."

"Oh, no!" wailed Teresa. "You really did save me from those terrible bandits!"

He shook his head and said, "Not exactly. They made sure we had no guns and gave us a chance to get you out of that hut you were supposed to be a prisoner in. I'm sorry I hit that so-called rapist so hard, or was he for real? Some of the gang might not have been fed the whole story, dumb as they looked."

She sobbed. "You know you saved me, just in the nick of time!"

He shrugged and said, "Sloppy way to run a railroad, but what the hell. Whatever we did, we didn't get to finish rescuing you. Another gang wiped out your friends and drafted us into the Nicaraguan army for a while. Am I talking too fast for you, Señora Montalban?"

"No, go ahead, this is getting interesting, Dick."

"Okay, once the so-called kidnapper's confederates were dead and Teresa was really missing, they didn't know what the hell to do. Old Pedro did the dumbest thing he could. He tried to pick up the ransom, anyhow, and we all know what happened to *him*. Teresa, here, made up a story about house servants drugging her. Since that was a lot of bull, we can assume that all the important plotters are out of action. It was a little complicated getting your long-lost child back here tonight, but suffice it to say we did. We were supposed to deliver her to Don Alberto and back up her charges that you were behind her abduction. The clues all pointed the other way. The people of this household all seemed to be good guys while all the known bad guys worked for Teresa, but she does tell a convincing story, and until you walked in just now to drop the last pieces of the puzzle in place, I'll have to admit that I was still a bit confused. Not sold but, yeah, confused. The Melina I was expecting to meet acts so stupid, she could have been up to anything.''

The real Melina smiled at him and asked, ''Do I seem intelligent to you, Dick?''

He nodded and said, ''Yeah. Even if you looked dumb, that diamond necklace alone is worth way more than the kidnappers figured to have to share at least a dozen ways. I hope you're *really* smart, though. Because now we'd better talk about the way this story ends.''

Teresa pointed a finger at Captain Gringo and wailed, ''Do not listen to his lies, Melina! He raped me too!''

Melina sighed and said, ''Oh, shut up. How do you think the story should end, Dick?''

''Teresa lies good. She'll say anything you tell her to say, to save her own neck. It's your move, Señora.''

Melina stared thoughtfully down at the now very frightened Teresa. She murmured, ''It would break my husband's heart to hear that his own granddaughter could be such a dreadful little sneak. I do not imagine that he would like to hear about her being raped by anyone, do you?''

''I don't think he'd even want to hear she'd been kissed. But should anyone ever twist my arm, I guess I'll have to tell them what she did with another woman too.''

Gaston protested from the doorway, ''Teresa, you never told me while *we* were making love that you went in for that sort of thing!''

She could only stare at him in numb horror. Melina soothed, ''There, there, I feel sure we all agree that you caballeros rescued her from those awful people with her honor still intact. Since no ransom was ever paid, the monsters who abducted her are all dead, and the dear child's back safe and sound, so other details don't seem important, do they, Teresa, darling?"

The girl stared up at the woman she hated, licked her lips, and asked, "You do not intend to accuse me when my grandfather returns, Melina, dear?"

"Why should I? He is my husband, and despite what you may think of me, I do not wish him to suffer a stroke or, in truth, even to feel less than love for his only grandchild. So now that we have all agreed on our story, perhaps we can allow the matter to rest there, eh? You were abducted by treacherous servants, these kind caballeros rescued you unharmed, and that, as they say, shall be that."

Teresa leapt up, dropped to her knees at Melina's feet, and wrapped her arms around the older woman's legs, sobbing with relief. The cool blonde said, "Let's not get sickening about this, you silly little snip. I said we could forget it, not that I *liked* you one bit, and from now on, when I shout froggy, dear Teresa, you had better be prepared for to jump!"

Shoving the near hysterical girl away, the Junoesque blonde turned to Captain Gringo and said, "Now that that is settled, you will no doubt wish to remain here until Don Alberto returns."

He said, "We can go back to our posada for now, señora. If he wants to say thanks, he can always find us there."

She shook her blond head firmly and insisted, "No. I wish for you to be here when he returns. I think I can control this brat now, but if I can't and have to change my story, I shall need someone to back me up."

From the floor Teresa wailed, "I will never try for to get you in trouble again, Melina!"

But the older woman said, "You had better not. I still trust you as I trust a very stupid snake. Will you not stay, cabelleros? I assure you we will do everything to make you feel welcome."

The soldiers of fortune exchanged glances. Gaston said, "We may not be able to get our old rooms at the posada back in any case." So Captain Gringo said, "Well, since you put it that way, señora, a night in a real bed won't hurt us, for a change."

She moved over to a bellpull to ring for servants, and the next thing they knew, they were enjoying a full course meal, four-star brandy, and some of Don Alberto's expensive perfectos. Their hostess told them to help themselves to extra smokes for later. So they did.

She sent Teresa off to bed first, like the naughty child she was, and tried again to reach her husband in the highlands by phone. It was no go. His train hadn't arrived yet.

She sighed and ordered her servants to show them up to separate guest rooms or, rather, apartments. Captain Gringo enjoyed a long, hot soak in a marble tub, then dried himself with a real Turkish towel and climbed between the sheets— silk, of course—of a big four-poster. He switched off the electric bed lamp. He still felt wide-awake. He didn't know why. The smooth silk sheets felt sexy as hell against his bare skin, but it wasn't as if he should be feeling hard up after all he'd been through lately.

But he was. He rolled belly down. It was a bad move. The soft silk-covered mattress reminded him of old Tobasca's whalelike charms. He wondered who was aboard them tonight. That was no way to get rid of a hard-on.

He was saved from more shameful methods when the bedroom door popped open and the ceiling light flashed on. He knew he'd locked the door. He knew where he'd placed his .38 before retiring too. But as he groped for it he saw that it was Melina Montalban, and the key in her hand explained some of it.

It didn't explain lots more. She was still wearing beige silk and diamonds. But she was putting the key in a pocket of her silk kimono, and as she shut the door behind her and twisted the latch, he saw that her latest outfit was open almost to her belly button and that she'd hung a smaller diamond pendant between her Junoesque ivory breasts. She'd let her hair down too. Apparently in more ways than one. She was trying to remain serene, but her breathing was a bit labored as she told him, "I just spoke to Don Alberto on the telephono. He is naturally delighted about Teresa's rescue and insists that you stay here with us until he can get back to thank you properly."

Captain Gringo propped himself up on one elbow, hoping to hide the bulge in the bedding below his waist, and said, "No problem. I can't think of a place I'd rather be right now. Did he, ah, say when he'd be arriving?"

"Alas, not before noon tomorrow. He intends to stay the night at Teresa's rancho in the high country and return after a good night's sleep. He said something about discussing matters with the local military while he is up that way. They were afraid Teresa might be with some banditos they have been searching for without much luck. They would no doubt be the people you rescued his granddaughter from in the end, no?"

"Probably. No sense changing the story more than we have to."

She nodded, moved over, and perched on the edge of his bed as she said, "I just explained that to Teresa. We have had quite a talk about the way things must be from now on, if she knows what is good for her. I have assured her that she will not starve should something happen to my husband. She in turn says she sees the advantages of obeying a loving older relation."

"I figured she might. Just how loving are you, Melina? Has anyone ever told you you have a great build?"

She dimpled and replied, "I could not help noticing your shoulders when first we met, Dick. But before we discuss such matters, forgive me, I am curious about your obvious quick wits. I know I am beautiful. Everyone has always said so. But you said you knew at a glance that I was not the sort of person Teresa tried so hard for to convince you I was. May I ask how you knew so quickly? Teresa is attractive, too, and a much better liar."

He chuckled and said, "There's no contest there. The story she and her pals tried to sell me from the beginning was convincing as hell. They even let Gaston and me figure some things out ourselves. That's the mark of a slick con artist. Are you sure you can handle the slippery little thing?''

"I think so. At the moment your friend the Frenchman will be handling her the rest of the night. I told her it was her duty to make a guest feel comfortable, whether she wanted to or not.''

She wasn't making *him* feel comfortable at all. But he managed a crooked smile as he told her, "You sure have odd ideas of punishment, Melina. I don't know if it's true what they say about *all* Frenchman, but it is about Gaston, so I doubt she'll feel much pain.''

The cool blonde nodded gravely and said, "I did not order her to Gaston's room as punishment, though it may serve to show her who is in charge of this family now. You obviously know something of our Spanish views about honor. So the more men she's been dishonored by, the less she may have to talk about, eh?''

He laughed and said, "I've heard about iron fists in velvet gloves, but you're something special.''

"I know. You still have not told me how you knew at a glance that we could trust one another, Dick.''

He said, "Oh, that was easy. I'd already wondered why a lady who just had to sit tight and inherit it all wanted to putz around with a ten-thousand-dollar deal. That's a lot more money down here than it is where I come from. I guess her confederates thought it was big money. But the minute I spotted jewelry that had to come from some place like Cartier or Tiffany . . .''

"I buy my jewelry from Fabergé, and by the way, it is my own. I was married before, to a very rich man. So I did not marry Don Alberto for his money, as you may have been told.''

"I didn't know that, and I didn't know you shop at the same place as the czar of all the Russias. But I could see you weren't a lady who thought ten lousy grand was real money. I didn't know if you were as smart as you looked or not, at first. But I knew you had to be smarter than the dumb blonde they tried to use as your stand-in, and as soon as I saw that I'd been duped with a ringer, it wasn't hard to figure why. The whole frame was pretty clumsy. But what the hell, if it had been good, it would have worked. You sure are an easygoing kid, Melina. Lots of ladies might not have taken it so calm.''

She shrugged and said, ''It was not my first impulse. I am grateful to you for suggesting a way to settle the whole distressing matter without causing further distress to my poor husband.''

He had to think about that. From his angle of advantage he could see one dusky-rose nipple peeking out at him, erect with desire. He said, casually, ''I guess you care a lot for your husband, huh?''

She said simply, ''I love Don Alberto, as a daughter loves a kindly father. It is not his fault that he is old and not, well, as healthy as *we* are.''

He said that sounded reasonable and reached for her. She didn't resist as he pulled her into bed with him, but as he moved to kiss her, she placed a gentle finger to his lips and said, ''Not yet. I make no secret and feel no shame for my desires. But in truth my main reason for coming here was to discuss just what we mean to tell Don Alberto when he arrives.''

''Is that why you came in dressed for bed, Melina?''

She never fluttered a lash—and he liked that—as she told him, ''I knew we would wind up having sex together before I left. We have much to talk about, and I confess that some of the things Teresa told me as we were agreeing on *her* story may have led me to wonder if you could possibly be as good and, ah, proportioned, as that ungrateful child says.''

He said, ''Let's find out. We've got all night to talk.''

She didn't resist but lay calmly back as he unfastened her robe to expose her Junoesque charms to the overhead light. Her soft brown eyes sparkled like the diamond in the hollow of her throat as he lowered his lips to hers. She kissed back warmly, putting her tongue to his, and didn't flinch as he ran his free hand down her lush curves to part the blond thatch between her shapely thighs. As he mounted her she spread her thighs wide to take all he had to offer and began to move in time with his thrusts, her soft hands caressing his back as she gave him what could best be described as a friendly old-fashioned fuck.

Melina didn't moan or groan or mutter words she might not mean in the cold gray dawn. He knew she was climaxing with him when her skin flushed a delicate pink from nipples to neck. But as he came and went limp atop her, Melina just stroked his spine fondly and said, "That was lovely. I would like to do it some more, as soon as we are rested. I told Teresa not to admit being more than a firm but fair employer to that horrid Pedro and . . . what do you find so amusing, Dick?"

He said, "You. I could swear you were conning me too, if I didn't have the lights on and if there was any reason for you to be doing this for ulterior motives."

She raised her legs to lock her ankles comfortably around his waist as she replied, "I told you for why I wish to spend the night making love to you, Dick. I have normal desires, you are a very handsome man in every way, and it is most difficult for a woman in my position to enjoy her carnal appetites discreetly. I knew, as soon as I could tell that you were a man who could keep a secret, that I wished for to lay you. Now that I have, I must say you give me more pleasure than I had the right to expect."

"You're some yum yum too. But this is only recreation to you, like having dinner with me?"

She dimpled up at him, contracted her lush insides teasingly, and said, "This feels more like a very sweet dessert. I wish for another helping or more. But let us not spoil it with mock words of love. I told you the only man I love is my dear and good husband. You and I can never be more than friends, and once he gets back to town, we can never be this friendly again, agreed?"

He started moving in her slow and sensuously, in time with

her languid vaginal contractions, as he said, "I get the picture. Do you mind if we make the most of this while we can?"

"Oh, I wish you would. Could you move a little faster, dear friend?"

He could. He shoved a pillow under her hips and spread her wider than before to long-dong her as she closed her eyes and took it with a soft smile of pleasure, as if she were an angel being patted on her wings. But she twisted and ground her firm hips like an imp in heat.

When they'd climaxed again that way, she still wanted to talk. Some dames were like that. It was hard to kiss and talk at the same time, and it was impossible to stop kissing any woman so beautiful if a guy had his face anywhere near hers. So he suggested another position, and when she said she wasn't familiar with it, she let him show her.

He got her on her hands and knees across the bed and rose to brace his bare feet on the expensive rug as she said, "Oh, I see. This *is* the position horses and other animals do it in, now that I think of it. I did not know we humans could do it this way. Our limbs are not the same length and . . . oh, I see we *can*! How interesting!"

He found it interesting indeed as he entered her from behind with a palm braced on either creamy buttock. She arched her spine and reclined her upper body on the mattress as she calmly went on talking. He laughed. It sure was a comfortable position for a conversation. He admired a woman who could enjoy sex like a man and just *do* it, without a lot of innocent protests. So as they humped like critters they discussed their co-conspiracy, if that was what it was. He had to admit that her approach to adultery was designed to hurt as few people as possible.

Great minds seemed to be running in the same channels as he plumbed her delicious depths. Melina sighed and asked, "Could we not try for to make it last this time, Dick? I know all good things must end, but I love what you are doing to my end right now."

He slowed down, teasing them both with long, luxurious strokes as he parted her cheeks with his thumbs for a better view of the inspiring scene. She said, "Oh, perfecto," then added in a more conversational tone, "When I spoke to my husband on the telephono, he told me to take good care of you until he returned and to meanwhile sound you out as to what you feel you and Gaston may have coming to you."

He shoved it in as far as it would go and replied, "I've seldom been taken care of better, and I'm sure Gaston's coming almost as good about now."

She said, "Thank you. It is good to know for certain I am a better lay than Teresa. But you did more than lay that wicked child. You completely fucked up her wicked plans. So even if we never tell her grandfather all the details, you deserve to be rewarded, my hero."

He had to start moving faster in her as he explained, "I only did what had to be done to save what was left of my reputation. I never signed a contract with Don Alberto, and by the time Gaston and I shot our way out, we were both a bit ahead financially. So what the hell, let's just settle for a little old kiss or something."

She gasped. "Oh, what you are doing is really something, and I have no doubt we shall get to kiss one another all over before this night must end. But I told you this was not an expression of gratitude, grateful as you are making me feel right now. So at *some* sane moment before my husband returns we simply must discuss the cash award you deserve for all you have done for this family!"

He laughed like hell and marveled aloud in time with his thrusts. "Jesus H. Christ, after all I've done and still *intend* to do for this family, I'm supposed to expect *money* too?"

More *Renegade*
by Ramsay Thorne

___#28 **THE SLAVE RAIDERS**
> (C32-398, U.S.A., $2.50)
> (C32-399, Canada, $3.25)

___#29 **PERIL IN PROGRESO**
> (C32-400, U.S.A., $2.50)
> (C32-401, Canada, $3.25)

___#30 **MAYHEM AT MISSION BAY**
> (C32-402, U.S.A., $2.50)
> (C32-403, Canada, $3.25)

___#31 **SHOOTOUT IN SEGOVIA**
> (C32-404, U.S.A., $2.50)
> (C32-405, Canada, $3.25)

___#32 **DEATH OVER DARIEN**
> (C32-407, U.S.A., $2.50)
> (C32-406, Canada, $3.25)

Renegade by Ramsay Thorne

WARNER BOOKS
P.O. Box 690
New York, N.Y. 10019

Please send me the books I have checked. I enclose a check or money order (not cash), plus 50¢ per order and 50¢ per copy to cover postage and handling.* (Allow 4 weeks for delivery.)

_____ Please send me your free mail order catalog. (If ordering only the catalog, include a large self-addressed, stamped envelope.)

Name _____

Address _____

City _____

State _____ Zip _____

*N.Y. State and California residents add applicable sales tax.　　11

And More From
MAX BRAND

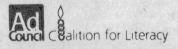